**"What are you waiting for?
For everything to be perfect?"**

Tory knew she was pushing Slade, but this was important to Mindy.

"I just don't want her hurt anymore. Last month we went shopping at the mall and a couple of children laughed at Mindy when she walked by. I don't want that to happen to her at school."

"God only gives us what we can handle."

"Mindy has handled enough for an eight-year-old."

"She asked to go to church with me on Sunday. She said she used to go with you and your wife, but not since the accident."

"Things have been so hectic and—" He paused, inhaled a deep breath and continued. "No, that's not quiet true. I feel God has let my family down. He took away Mindy's mother. He took away who my daughter was. She's had to start over, relearning the simplest things. What kind of God puts a child through that? Why couldn't it have been me?"

Books by Margaret Daley

Love Inspired

The Power of Love #168
Family for Keeps #183
Sadie's Hero #191
The Courage To Dream #205
What the Heart Knows #236
A Family for Tory #245

MARGARET DALEY

feels she has been blessed. She has been married for thirty-three years to her husband, Mike, whom she met in college. He is a terrific support and her best friend. They have one son, Shaun, who married his high school sweetheart in June 2002.

Margaret has been writing for many years and loves to tell a story. When she was a little girl, she would play with her dolls and make up stories about their lives. Now she writes these stories down. She especially enjoys weaving stories about families and how faith in God can sustain a person when things get tough. When she isn't writing, Margaret is fortunate to be a teacher for students with special needs. She has taught for over twenty years and loves working with her students. She has also been a Special Olympics coach and has participated in many sports with her students.

A FAMILY FOR TORY

MARGARET DALEY

Love Inspired®

Published by Steeple Hill Books™

STEEPLE HILL BOOKS

ISBN 0-373-87255-0

A FAMILY FOR TORY

This edition published by arrangement with Steeple Hill Books.

Visit us at www.steeplehill.com

Printed in U.S.A.

So that we may boldly say, The Lord is my helper,
and I will not fear what man shall do unto me.

—*Hebrews* 13:6

To the people I work with,
especially Terri, Rene, Katie, Becky, Anne, Laurie,
Naomai, Mike, Lila, Stacie, Debbie, Lisa—
you all make coming to work each day special.

Chapter One

Slade Donaldson switched off the engine and glanced toward his eight-year-old daughter. ''Ready, Mindy? Are you sure you want to do this? I'll be gone for about an hour.''

Mindy nodded, her face brightening with a huge grin. ''Tor-ee needs—my—uh—help, Dad-dy.''

Every time he heard his daughter struggle to say something, his heart twisted into a knot that he feared would never unravel. ''Then I'd better meet this Tory Alexander.'' Since his housekeeper had taken Mindy to her physical therapy for the past few months, he'd never met the woman who had brought her pony into the hospital to cheer up the children and captured his daughter's interest.

Mindy pointed toward a petite woman emerging from a barn, leading a horse on a rein. ''Th—ere.'' Her grin widened, her brown eyes sparkling.

''Then let's go. I need to be at the bank in twenty

minutes for my meeting.'' He thrust open his car door, then hurried around to help his daughter.

''I can—do—this.'' Mindy pulled herself to a standing position using the door.

The tightness in his chest made his breathing difficult. He offered his daughter his arm. She clasped it to steady herself, then began to make her way toward the woman by the opening into the barn. Two weeks ago his daughter had declared she didn't want to use her walker anymore. Each day since, Mindy had leaned less and less on him as she'd walked. Progress, Slade thought, due partly to this woman before him. She and her pony, Mirabelle, have been the reasons Mindy tolerated her physical therapy at the hospital over the past few months. He was in Tory Alexander's debt.

Tory saw Mindy approaching and tied the reins to the fence of the riding ring. Then she strode toward the girl with a smile of greeting. Slade was surprised by how small the woman was. The horse she'd been leading was at least seventeen hands tall, towering over her. Her long auburn hair was swept back in a ponytail with a few stray strands curling around her oval face. Freckles sprinkled her turned-up nose and her large brown eyes drew a person to her. Fringed in dark lashes, Slade felt their pull as she came to a stop only a few feet from Mindy and him.

Tory looked at his daughter. ''I'm so glad you didn't have to cancel, Mindy.'' Then she turned those large brown eyes on him. ''I'm sorry to hear about Mrs. Watson's emergency. Will her niece be okay?''

''She just went into labor a little early. My housekeeper assures me everything will be all right and she'll be back in a week or so."

"That's good to hear. I know she was excited about her niece's pregnancy. First in the family." Tory lifted her arm toward Mindy to take over being her support if she needed. "Come on, Mindy. Let's show your father the barn."

"I have a meeting I need to go to."

"Dad-dy, just—" Mindy swallowed several times "—see Bel-le."

Slade stared at his daughter's face, lit with hope and eagerness, and he couldn't refuse the invitation even though it would make him late. After all, she was the reason he worked fourteen-hour days. He wanted only the best care for Mindy, and that cost money. "Lead the way." Sweeping his arm toward the barn, he followed the pair.

As he entered, surprisingly the only scents to assail him were hay and leather. Scanning the darker interior, he noticed how clean the barn was. A few stalls had horses in them but most were empty. "Where are your horses?"

"In the pastures."

"How many do you have?"

"Fifteen and one pony, Mirabelle, or, as Mindy loves to call her, Belle."

"Th-ere," Mindy said, gesturing toward the last stall. She hurried her pace, her left foot dragging in the dirt.

Mindy stumbled. Slade lurched forward to catch her, but Tory had already steadied her. Mindy continued her fast pace toward Mirabelle, towing Tory behind her.

Tory quickened her step to keep up. "Whoa. Mirabelle isn't going anywhere."

"Haven't seen—her in—lo-ong time."

Slade scooped Mindy up in his arms and continued toward the stall at the very end of the barn. "It's only been five days, sweetie."

"Too lo-ong."

While Tory swung the stall door open, he went inside with Mindy. She squirmed.

"Dad-dy, put me down."

He settled his daughter in front of Mirabelle and kept his hands on her shoulders so she wouldn't fall as she found her balance. Even though her surgery had been eight months before, it was still hard for her to keep her equilibrium at times.

She bent forward and threw her arms around the pony's neck. Nuzzling the animal, Mindy giggled. "Isn't she ugly? No—" she shook her head "—pretty?"

Slade inspected the pony's golden brown coat and big brown eyes that suddenly reminded him of Mirabelle's owner. "Very pretty."

"You know Mirabelle has been waiting just for you so you could give her a good brushing. No one does it better." Tory produced a curry comb and passed it to Mindy.

Tory helped Mindy position herself so she could start on the pony's left side. With one hand clutching the mane, Mindy began her task. Tory stepped back toward the entrance, motioning for Slade to follow.

Outside the stall she paused. Reluctantly Mindy's dad joined her.

"Do you think we should leave her alone like that?" he asked, a frown creasing his brow.

"She'll be fine. She's done that half a dozen times now and loves to. It's her private time with Mirabelle." A giggle drifted to her, and Tory smiled. "See. I think she tells Belle her secrets."

"What secrets?" Panic laced his question.

"All little girls have them. Who's her favorite movie star? What songs does she like? Who's her best friend at school?"

"She didn't go to school this year. She's being tutored at home."

"Is she going to attend in the fall?"

Slade opened his mouth to answer, then clamped it shut. He glanced away. "I don't know. It depends on her therapy and how fast she recovers."

"Mindy's so good with the other children who come for riding lessons. She misses her friends."

Slade straightened, his jaw clenched. "I won't have her go to school and be teased because she talks too slow and walks funny."

"Kids can be very accepting."

"And kids can be very cruel. Mindy's gone through so much this past year because of the car accident that took her mother and caused her epilepsy."

"But didn't the surgery make the epilepsy better?"

"She hasn't had a seizure, but at what cost?" Slade waved his hand toward the stall where his daughter was talking to the pony, frustration in every taut line of his body.

"Do you regret agreeing to the surgery?"

Slade plowed his fingers through his hair. "Yes—no. The doctors told me this was best for Mindy, that given time she would recover most of her speech and physical abilities. A few years from now we'll hardly know she had part of her brain removed."

"But it doesn't make it any easier right now?"

"No," he clipped out.

"I didn't mean to intrude, but Mindy has become very important to me. I was hoping she could come more often to the stables to help out. She asked me to talk to you about it."

"She did? When?"

"She called me this morning and asked."

"So that's who she was talking to on the phone. I thought it was one of her girlfriends. When I made that assumption, she didn't correct me."

"She wants to be my assistant and go with me to the hospital when I take Mirabelle next time."

Slade relaxed the tensed set to his shoulders. "It's hard for me to say no when Mirabelle is the reason my daughter would cheerfully go to the hospital for her physical therapy. Before Mirabelle, Mrs. Watson and I had a horrible time getting Mindy to go. Now with the promise of seeing the pony, she'll do just about anything."

"Animals can be great therapy for people. That's why I started my riding stable for people in need, especially children. So what do you say about Mindy helping me out?"

"Let me think about it. That's asking you to do a lot for Mindy."

"I don't mind. If I didn't want her to be my helper, I wouldn't have asked."

"Still..." Slade checked his watch. "I'd better get going. I'm already late as it is. I'll be back in an hour."

"We'll be in the riding ring."

Slade strode toward his car, feeling the touch of Tory's gaze on his back. It took a supreme effort not to turn around and look at her. She was an attractive lady who obviously loved animals and children. Very appealing qualities in a woman, he thought, then shook his head. What in the world was he thinking? After this past twenty-two months piecing his life back together, he didn't think he could deal with anything that required his emotions be involved. He had all he could handle with Mindy and her recovery. But first, he had to secure the loan for the second phase of the expansion of his company.

"You're doing great, Mindy. Sit up straight. Take command." Tory watched the young girl walk her horse around the riding ring. The child's face glowed, her proud expression attesting to one of the reasons Tory spent so much time and money on her Bright Star Stables—the looks on her riders' faces when they were successful. "Okay, Mindy, that's it for today. You need to cool Paint down now."

"Dad-dy say yes?"

Tory assisted Mindy in dismounting, then handed

the child the reins. ‘‘He’s going to think about you helping me at the hospital with Mirabelle.’’

The girl’s lower lip stuck out in a pout. ‘‘Why?’’

‘‘Because your day is full as it is. With your schooling and therapies, Mindy, you don’t have a lot of extra time.’’

The sudden sound of Slade’s voice made Tory stiffen. The erratic beat of her heart crashed against her chest. With her attention totally focused on Mindy, Tory hadn’t heard him approaching. She didn’t like being caught unaware. It emphasized her vulnerability. Swinging around toward him, she took in his tall height, over six feet, and muscular frame that even his suit couldn’t conceal. She stamped down her alarm. This was Mindy’s father.

The little girl gripped Tory’s arm and twisted about to face her father who stopped a few feet from her. ‘‘Summer—is al-most—here. No sch-ool then.’’

One of Slade’s dark brows arched. ‘‘Who said that?’’

‘‘No va-va-ca-tion?’’

‘‘You’ll have one, a short one. But you have some catching up to do, young lady.’’

Mindy sighed heavily. ‘‘I can’t—’’ The young girl paused and swallowed several times ‘‘—help Tor-ee?’’

‘‘No, I didn’t say that.’’

A bright gleam shone in Mindy’s eyes. ‘‘I can!’’

‘‘I didn’t say that, either. I’m still thinking about it.’’

Instantly the child’s expression crumbled and her shoulders sagged.

"Take care of your horse and let me talk with Tory for a minute. I won't be long."

Mindy led Paint toward the barn, her left foot leaving a drag mark in the dirt. The little girl's head was lifted. Tory had been working the past month on instilling confidence into the child, something that had suffered after her operation.

The second Mindy disappeared into the barn, Tory swung around, prepared to defend her reasons for wanting the girl to work with her. Slade cut her off with "Mindy won't make her next lesson."

His words took the steam out of her. Surprised, she grappled for something to say. "Why?" was all she could manage to think of.

"With Mrs. Watson gone I don't have the time to bring her out here next Tuesday. As it is, I'm having a hard time getting help to take care of Mindy while my housekeeper's away. I thought today I had everything arranged, but my arrangements fell through."

"I can help," Tory said without really thinking through the consequences. But she adored the child and didn't want her to miss her twice-weekly riding lessons.

"I couldn't ask you—"

"You didn't. I volunteered to help. Mindy wants to spend more time here. I could use her help and watch her at the same time. It's perfect for everyone."

Slade shook his head, deep lines in his forehead. "But—"

Tory held up her hand to stop his flow of words.

"Who are you going to get to sit with Mindy? Someone from a baby-sitting organization? Mindy and I are buddies. I would love to help her out. I wouldn't offer if I didn't mean it."

"I don't know how long Mrs. Watson is going to be gone. Everything happened so suddenly. She said a week or maybe longer."

"One thing I've learned taking care of animals is to go with the flow. One day at a time. Don't worry. The future will take care of itself." At least that was what she was counting on. Because right now she wasn't sure how long she could keep Bright Star Stables operational.

"Not without a lot of help from me." He took a deep breath and blew it out between pursed lips. "Okay. If you're sure."

"I am."

"Then I'll bring her first thing Monday morning."

"What time?"

Slade peered toward the barn, his eyes narrowing as though he were trying to see into the dark shadows. "I'm afraid seven. I have an eight o'clock meeting I need to attend."

"That's fine by me. I'm usually up by five. I'll have the stalls clean by that time." Mindy's presence reinforced all the reasons she worked long hours to keep Bright Star Stables going.

"That's mighty ambitious."

"There's nothing ambitious about it. I'm usually the only one to do it. I depend on volunteers to help. Otherwise, this is a one man—or rather, woman—show."

"Thanks. You're a lifesaver." Slade stuck his hand out.

Tory stared at it for a brief moment, then fit her hand within his and quickly shook it before pulling back, taking a step away as she did.

"Hopefully Mrs. Watson will only be gone for a week."

"Don't worry about how long it will be."

The tense set to his shoulders relaxed. "Now that only leaves rearranging her speech and physical therapies next week."

"When are they?"

"Mindy has speech Monday afternoon at four and physical therapy Tuesday and Friday mornings."

"I need to come into town Monday. I can take her and you can pick her up there."

"I can't—"

"Didn't we just go through this? I know how important her therapies are for her and how hard it can be to rearrange. It's no big deal."

"Tor-ee, I'm fin-ished."

Tory swung around to watch as Mindy made her way toward them. Dirt dusted her cheeks with some bits of hay sticking out of her hair. "Are you all right?" she asked while Slade rushed toward Mindy.

The little girl waved her father away. "I'm o-kay. Just—fell, that's—all."

Slade looped his arm about Mindy's shoulders. "Are you hurt?"

Mindy shook her head, dislodging a piece of hay that floated to the ground.

"We should have brought your walker. This uneven surface—"

"No! I—I—hate it!"

"Your dad agreed to you helping me. In fact, you're going to be my assistant all next week while Mrs. Watson is gone."

"I am!" Mindy brushed the rest of the hay from her hair, a huge grin revealing a missing tooth. "Thanks, Dad-dy."

"You're welcome, sweetie."

"I get—to—miss—sch-ool?" The child's eagerness peppered the air with her enthusiasm.

"No way. I'll have your homebound teacher come out here for the week."

Some of Mindy's enthusiasm evaporated, a slump to her stance. "I hate—sch-ool—too."

"Mindy, we've had this discussion. School and your lessons are important." Slade held his arm out for his daughter to take, then he led her toward his car.

Tory followed, wishing she had the right to step in. She remembered when she was struggling to learn to read in elementary school. She'd hated school, too, until she had mastered her problem. Mindy had to fight hard to regain everything she'd once taken for granted, such as walking, talking, taking care of herself. It would be normal for her to feel that way about her lessons when she was still trying to recoup what she'd lost after the operation.

After securing Mindy into the front seat and closing the door, Slade moved toward the back of the car where Tory stood. "We've had this argument every week since the homebound teacher started. She remembers what she used to be able to do with ease. Now those things are so hard for her that she often becomes very frustrated.''

There was a part of Tory that wanted to reach out and touch this man in pain, but there was a part that held her frozen in place. ''She's come a long way in a short time.''

Dark shadows clouded his blue eyes. ''If I could trade places with Mindy, I would in a heartbeat. The worse thing for me is to have to stand by and watch her suffer.''

His whispered words held anguish in them. Tory lifted her hand toward him, her fingers trembling as they lay on his arm for a brief moment before slipping away. ''Prayer has always helped me through the difficult times.''

''Mindy was innocent. This should never have happened to her in the first place. She was perfectly normal until the car wreck. Why would God do this to her?''

The pain in his voice robbed Tory of her breath. The heaviness in her chest threatened to squeeze the air completely from her lungs.

He started to turn away, then swung back toward her. ''It's been a long week. I didn't mean to burden you with this. I'll bring Mindy out Monday morning.'' He offered her a fleeting smile, said, ''Thanks for all your help,'' then strode to the driver's side and slid behind the wheel.

As his car pulled out, Tory fought the tears quickly

filling her eyes. *Lord, help this man find his path back to You. He is hurting and needs Your comfort.*

"Wh-ere's—Dad-dy?" Mindy asked, worry furrowing her brow.

Tory glanced at her watch for the third time in ten minutes. "His meeting probably ran over. That's all. We'd better wait here for him."

"Ba-th-ro-oom." Mindy labored over the word, the lines in her face deepening.

"I'll wait out here in the reception area for your dad while you're gone."

"Be back." Mindy made her way across the room and disappeared through the door where clients went for their speech therapy.

Picking up a magazine, Tory began flipping through it, not really seeing the words on the page. Slade was fifteen minutes late. Why hadn't he called? What was wrong? She chewed on her lower lip, her own worry coming to the foreground. Finally she gave up trying to read the magazine and tossed it back on the table in front of her.

The outside door swung open, and Slade entered. He was all right, Tory thought, her gaze skimming down his length. Relief shimmered through her.

When he caught sight of her in the corner, he hurried to her and sat next to her. For just a second Tory's heart sped. She pressed her lips together to still her usual reaction to someone invading her space.

"I'm so sorry I was late. My cell phone is dead

so I couldn't call you to tell you that I was sitting in traffic waiting for them to clear up an accident."

"Anyone hurt?"

He frowned, his blue eyes dark. "Yes. It was a mess. They're still working on it."

"Dad-dy!"

Slade looked toward Mindy who stood a few feet away. The little girl launched herself at her father, throwing her arms around him.

"You oo-kay?" Mindy plastered herself against her father. "What—" She couldn't finish her sentence. Tears shone in her eyes and one slipped down her cheeks.

Slade smoothed his daughter's hair back from her face and kissed the top of her head. "I'm fine. Just delayed. I couldn't call. Sorry about that. I know how you are when I'm late."

"Su-re—okay?" Mindy sniffed.

He squeezed her to him. "Yes, sweetie."

"He just got stuck in traffic," Tory said as she rose and gathered up her purse.

"What—was—a mess?" Mindy leaned back to peer at her father.

Slade paled. "Nothing important."

"Dad-dy, what?"

He forced a laugh. "My day, sweetie, but not now. How about us taking Tory out to dinner? I think she deserves our thanks for helping us out."

"Yes!"

Mindy's excitement touched Tory. She'd always wanted children—lots of them—but didn't see how that goal was possible now. Slade was so lucky to have a daughter like Mindy. "How can I refuse?"

"You—can't." Mindy scooted off her father's lap and took Tory's hand, pulling her toward the door.

"I guess my daughter is hungry, even though it's not much after five. Do you mind an early dinner?"

Laughing at Mindy's eagerness to leave, Tory tossed back over her shoulder while the child was dragging her through the opened door, "I'm always hungry, so I can eat early or late or both. Where are we going? I can follow you in my truck."

"Leave your truck here and I'll bring you back for it afterward."

"I can follow—"

"Plee-ze," Mindy said, stopping in the middle of the parking lot.

"You make it hard to say no, young lady." Tory forced a scolding tone to her voice, but she was sure the smile that accompanied her words wiped out any threat.

"You—will?"

Tory looked toward Slade for help. He shrugged and shook his head. She was on her own. "I guess so. But wouldn't it be easier if I—"

At Slade's car while opening the back door, Mindy announced, "You—can—sit—" she paused, searching for her words "—in the front."

"No, that's—" Tory watched as the little girl hopped into the back seat faster than she had seen her move since she had known her.

Over the top of the car Tory spied Slade looking at her. "I guess I'll sit in front."

"Please. I draw the line at being a chauffeur."

When Slade started the engine and pulled out of the parking space, he asked, "Any favorite place you would like to go?"

"I'm not picky. Wherever you two like."

The second he maneuvered the car into the flow of traffic Mindy said, "Music—plee-ze."

Tory switched on the radio. She'd found Mindy loved to listen to it even while working in the barn.

The end of a popular song sounded over the radio, then the announcer came on. "Now for a traffic update. There has been a multicar wreck on—"

Slade switched the dial to Off. Surprised, Tory glanced at him. Then she heard the scream from the back seat.

Chapter Two

"Nooo!" Mindy screamed over and over.

Slade crossed two lanes of traffic to pull into an almost-deserted office parking lot. Before Tory had time to react to the situation, he was out of the car and thrusting open the back door.

He hauled his daughter into his arms and held her tightly to him, whispering, "It's okay, sweetheart. You're all right. I'm here. Nothing's going to hurt you ever again. I promise."

Tory twisted around, desperately wanting to help Mindy. She had come to love the child in the short time she'd known her. The child's sobs filled the air with her pain, a pain Tory wished she could wipe away.

"Mom-my," Mindy cried, her voice muffled by the blue cotton of Slade's shirt.

But Tory heard the pitiful wail and knew the announcer had triggered a memory of Mindy's own wreck that had changed the little girl's life forever.

Tory's heart pounded against her chest in slow, anguish-filled throbs, mirroring the distress in Mindy. Tory knew more than most how quickly life could change; one split second could make all the difference. If only she hadn't gone out.... Tory pushed the memory away, refusing to allow it into her mind. She couldn't alter the past, but with God's guidance, she could protect herself.

She caught Slade's attention and mouthed, "Can I help?"

He shook his head, stroking his daughter's back. "Sweetie, Mommy's gone. But I'm here for you."

"It—it—" Mindy struggled for her words. "It—hurt."

"I know, baby. But you're safe now."

Slade's eyes slid closed, but not before Tory saw their glistening sheen. Tears clogged Tory's throat and misted her own eyes. She blinked, trying to get a grip on her emotions that careened out of control.

Mindy shuddered and Slade clutched her tighter. "Mommy's watching over you, baby. Taking care of you. She'll always be with you in here." He laid his hand over his daughter's heart.

Helpless, Tory drew in deep breaths after deep breaths but still she ached for the pair. She felt as if she had intruded on a private family moment and should disappear. She would give anything to take the child's pain away, but from experience knew that was something another couldn't do.

Mindy pulled back, sniffing and wiping her nose. "I—" she sucked in a huge gulp of air "—know, Dad-dy."

He cupped his daughter's face in his large hands. "I love you, sweetie."

She sniffled again. "I know."

Slade brushed the pads of his thumbs across Mindy's cheeks, erasing all evidence of her tears. "Are you ready to show Tory a good time?" Tenderness marked his expression as he peered at his daughter with eyes a soft azure. "I thought we would go to your favorite restaurant."

"Goldie's?"

"Of course. Is there another?"

"No!" A grin split Mindy's face.

Slade kissed his daughter, then slipped from the back seat. When he settled behind the steering wheel and started the engine, he threw Tory a glance that caused her heart to flip over. Sadness mixed with a look of appeal for understanding. She slid her hand across the console, almost touching Slade in reassurance. At the last second she pulled back and smiled at him instead.

"I love Goldie's hamburgers and onion rings," Tory said to Mindy, trying to ignore the heat of a blush she felt creep up her face at Slade's intense regard.

"Me, too." Mindy clapped, her left hand curled so that her palms didn't meet.

"With everything on it, even onions."

Tory caught Slade's look. The smile that glinted in his eyes warmed her. Her blush deepened. Aware his gaze was still riveted to her, she shifted in the leather seat, crossing and uncrossing her ankles. Uncomfortable under his intense scrutiny, she searched for something to say. Silence dominated the small confines of the car. Nothing she thought seemed appropriate so she let the quiet reign.

Fifteen minutes later Slade drove into the parking lot next to Goldie's. After he assisted Mindy from the back seat, they all headed into the restaurant, decorated in homespun décor, reminiscent of a farmhouse, with the scent of baking bread and coffee saturating the air.

Tory sat across from Mindy and Slade in the booth along the large front window that overlooked a pond. Geese and ducks swam in the water, which drew the little girl's attention.

''Look—'' Mindy frowned, her brow wrinkled in thought ''—bab-ies.''

The fluency of the little girl's speech had improved over the months since Tory had known her, but still the child labored to put her words together, to find the correct word to say. Tory wanted to hug her for her perseverance.

''The last time Mindy and I were here, the geese were sitting on their nests. They're three couples and it looks like they have all had their babies. Now she'll want to come back every week to keep track of them.''

''I have a pond, Mindy, on my property. We'll have to ride there one day and have a picnic.''

''Dad-dy, too?''

Tory's gaze slid to Slade's. ''Do you ride?''

He laughed. ''Sort of.''

Tory arched one brow in question.

''The last time was in high school, so it's been

years since I've been on a horse. Is it like riding a bicycle?''

''Sort of.'' Tory downed a large swallow of ice water, her throat suddenly parched.

''Well, then, yes, I do ride—or let's just say I know how to fall gracefully when the horse bolts.''

''Now you've piqued my curiosity. What happened the last time you rode?''

''I had leaned over to open the gate into the pasture when my horse got spooked by a rabbit darting in front of him. He decided to take off, leaving me dangling from the gate.''

Mindy giggled. ''Oh, Dad-dy.''

''I've fallen a few times, too, and I can't always say they were graceful falls.'' Tory took another long sip of her water, relishing the cool liquid.

Slade started to say something when the waitress approached to take their orders. After she left, he grinned. ''When I fell, I landed in a mud puddle and was covered from head to toe. It was a *big* mud puddle.''

''When can—we—do it?'' Mindy asked, eagerness giving her face a radiant glow.

''How about this weekend? I'm free after church on Sunday.'' Tory glanced from the little girl to Slade.

''Only if you allow me to bring the picnic.''

''This is my treat. I invited you.''

''Then let me bring the dessert.'' Determination marked his expression.

Tory shrugged. ''Fine.''

''What do you like?''

"Oh, just about anything with chocolate. Surprise me."

"I've gotten the impression you weren't someone who liked to be surprised."

"Not usually." Tory clasped her hands in her lap to still their trembling. Control and order were so important in her life, the threads that held it together. "I don't like to take risks, either, but I think I'll be safe with you bringing the dessert."

"Isn't your Bright Star Stables a financial risk?"

"Yes, but then some things are important enough to risk. I saw a need and wanted to do something about it."

"And this parent is grateful. If I can help you with anything, please let me know."

Tory thought about her low bank account, but pride kept her from saying anything. For many years she had done everything on her own. She was used to that and would somchow make the therapeutic riding program a success. When her aunt's inheritance had allowed her to fulfill a dream, she'd known in her heart this was what God had wanted her to do with her life. God would provide the means to keep Bright Star Stables going.

Slade's gaze bore into her as if he could reach into her mind and read it. "It's okay to ask for help when you need it."

"Look—Dad-dy." Mindy jostled her father's arm, then pointed out the window at the baby geese swimming in a line behind one of their parents with the other bringing up the rear.

If it wouldn't have raised more questions at

Mindy's timely interruption, Tory would have gladly hugged and kissed the child. The conversation was getting too personal for her. Keeping people at a distance had become such a habit for her that any probing into her feelings or past proved highly uncomfortable. She swiped the film of perspiration from her upper lip, then finished off her cold water.

After watching the geese with his daughter for a few minutes, Slade returned his attention to Tory. "I'll drop the subject for now, but it's in my best interest to see Bright Star Stables continue."

Mindy swung her gaze to her father, a deep line across her forehead. "What's—wrong?"

With his regard trained on Tory, Slade answered, "Nothing, sweetheart. I just wanted Tory to know how much we both appreciate the work she does."

Mindy bounced up and down. "Yeah!"

Heat scorched her cheeks. She noticed a few patrons looking their way. Breaking eye contact with Slade, she studied her place mat. "Thank you," she whispered, relieved that the waitress brought them their food, taking the focus off her. She preferred being in the background, having had more than her share of the limelight in the past—something she never wanted to relive again.

Tory bit into her thick, juicy hamburger and sighed. "I'd forgotten how great this tasted." She popped a small onion ring into her mouth. "And this. Of course, this will go straight to my hips."

"I don't think that'll hurt you." Slade dumped several sugar packets into his iced tea.

"It will if I had to buy a whole new wardrobe.

About all I can afford is a flour sack.'' The second she'd said it, she regretted the reference to her financial state.

Slade's eyes gleamed, but his lips remained pressed together.

Tory blew out a breath of air, thankful he wasn't going to pursue the topic. ''Have you lived in Cimarron City long?''

''All my life. How about you?''

''Just a few years. I moved here from Dallas.''

''What made you leave Dallas for Oklahoma?''

She should have expected the question, but still it took her by surprise. ''The weather.''

''We have the same beastly heat in the summer as Dallas.''

''Actually, my aunt died and left me her small ranch. I came to sell it and decided to stay.''

''You don't miss the big city.''

''Cimarron City is big enough for me. Besides, I'm a country gal at heart, and even though there are eighty thousand living here, it doesn't seem that way when I'm out on my ranch.''

''But it's still a far cry from Dallas.''

And for that Tory was thankful, but didn't say it out loud. Her memories of her hometown of Dallas were laden with sorrow, which had nothing to do with the city itself. But if she never went back, that would suit her just fine. ''Do you have any other family here?'' She wanted to take the focus off her and Dallas.

''I have an uncle in a retirement home in Tulsa. His son moved away when he went to college and hasn't returned except to visit a few times. My younger brother lives in Chicago and loves the big city. My father died ten years ago and Mom decided to live in the southernmost tip of Florida where it's warm all the time. So I'm the last Donaldson here in Cimarron City."

Mindy tugged on his arm. "Me—too."

"How right you are. Mindy and I are the last Donaldsons here. How about your family?"

Tory finished another huge onion ring, then washed it down with a swallow of raspberry-flavored tea. "All my family lives in Texas."

"Do you see them much?"

"They visit the ranch every summer for the Fourth of July."

"You don't go home?"

"It's hard for me to get away because of the horses. Someone has to look after them and I can't afford help. I'm stuck, but I don't mind."

"Are all the horses at the ranch yours?" Slade took a bite of his hamburger.

"No, I stable some. That brings me some needed income to do what I love."

"The therapeutic riding program?"

Tory nodded. "I'll need to get back to the ranch before dark. I still have some chores to do."

"Are you through, Mindy?" Slade tossed his napkin on the table.

The little girl gulped down the rest of her chocolate milk.

"Yep," she said, displaying a creamy brown mustache.

Slade took her napkin and wiped her mouth. "We'd better go. You have a big day tomorrow. You've got physical therapy in the morning."

Mindy pouted. "Do—I—have to?"

"It won't be long, sweetie, before you won't have to. But for now, yes."

After paying for the dinner, Slade escorted Mindy and Tory to his car. Twenty minutes later, he pulled into the parking lot at the speech therapist's office.

He glanced at Mindy in the back seat and smiled. "She still falls asleep riding in the car when she's exhausted."

"She worked hard today at the barn. She also rode." Tory pushed her door open and was surprised when she saw Slade get out of the car, too. "I'm only parked a few feet away."

"I know," he said, coming around the front of his car. "But I felt I owed you an explanation about what happened earlier with Mindy. And I don't want her waking up and overhearing."

The spring air cooled Tory's cheeks and the soft wind blew stray strands of her hair about her face. She brushed them behind her ears, the scent of freshly mowed grass lacing the breeze. "You don't need to explain anything." She moved the few feet to her truck door, aware of Slade's presence in every fiber of her being. She clutched the handle.

"After the accident, I couldn't get Mindy to ride in a car for months. Finally she does, now, but any mention of a car wreck and she falls apart. I try to shelter her from hearing about any accidents, but sometimes I can't."

''Like today when she was listening to the radio.''

''She loves to listen to music. She usually listens to CDs.''

''But I turned the radio on before you could put a CD in. I'm so sorry. I didn't know. I was just trying to help since you were focused on driving.''

He took a step toward her. Her heart skipped a beat. She plastered her back against her door, her hands tightening into fists.

''We've always listened to the radio while doing the chores in the barn,'' she said, needing to talk to take her mind off his nearness.

''I'm not telling you to make you upset. I just wanted you to know some of the things that Mindy is still coping with.''

''Is there anything else? I don't want to be the cause of any more anxiety.''

''She still wakes up from nightmares. Thankfully not lately. I'm hoping those are behind her.'' He raked both hands through his hair, a look of anguish on his face. ''Because frankly I have a hard time coping with seeing my daughter like that.''

''From what I saw back there, you did a wonderful job of reassuring her. That's all you can do.'' The hammering of her heart eased as the conversation centered on Mindy.

''Is it? There should be something else I can do to make things better for Mindy.'' Rubbing one hand along the back of his neck, he rolled his shoulders to relax the tension gripping him.

But Tory saw its continual grasp on him in his taut stance and the grim lines craving his expression.

"Being there for Mindy is the most important thing you can do."

"The wreck should never have happened. If only—"

Instantly, without thought, Tory started to lay her fingers over his mouth to still his words. She froze in midaction, her eyes widening. His gaze riveted to hers. For a few seconds everything came to a standstill.

Dropping her arm to her side, she said in a strained voice, "It doesn't do us any good to think about the what-ifs. We can't change the past. We can only influence the present."

"Live for today? Forget about the past?"

"Right." If only she could heed her own advice. She was trying, but there were times it was so difficult.

"Have you been successful doing that?"

She forced a smile. "I'm working on it."

"In other words, no."

Tory yanked open her truck door. "I'd better be going. I still have a lot of things to do before dark." She escaped into the quiet of her pickup, determined to keep her eyes trained forward. But even though she didn't look at Slade, she felt his probing observation delve deep inside, seeking answers about her past, something she guarded closely and never wanted to relive. And above all, certainly didn't want to share with anyone.

Quickly she backed out of the parking space, and as she pulled out into traffic, she chanced a glance at Slade. He stood where she had left him, a bewildered look on his face. After that evasive move, she wondered if he would bring Mindy tomorrow to the ranch.

Out on her front porch Tory eased herself into the old rocker and raised her glass of iced tea to press it against her heated face. The coldness felt wonderful after Tory had spent most of the day doing the work of two people. She needed to hire someone to help her, but that just wasn't possible at the moment, especially after the notice she'd received from the bank today.

Resting her head, she closed her eyes and continued to roll the glass over her flushed skin. At least Slade brought Mindy out late this morning. The child's cheerful attitude was a balm that soothed those long hours of work and her fretting over where the money for the loan was going to come from. With Mindy next to her, she repaired the fence in one pasture and even had time for the child to ride this afternoon after the three o'clock lesson. Every day Mindy was improving, self-confident when she handled the new mare.

When Tory thought about the little girl eagerly handing her the nails for the fence, Tory's heart swelled. She wanted children so badly—her niece and nephew weren't enough. Even the children she taught didn't fulfill the void in her heart. It was that simple and that complex. She released a long sigh and finally took a sip of her drink.

A scream rent the air. Tory bolted to her feet, the glass crashing to the wooden planks of the porch.

Leaping over the mess, she rushed for the door and wrenched it open as another scream vibrated down her length.

In the living room Mindy sat ramrod straight on the couch with her eyes so huge that was all Tory could focus on. She was at the child's side in an instant that seemed to take forever.

Hugging Mindy to her, she murmured, "What's wrong, baby?"

"I—I—" The child tried to drag air into her lungs, but she couldn't seem to get a decent breath.

"Take it easy. Relax. One breath at a time, Mindy." Tory willed her voice to stay calm while inside she quaked, the beat of her pulse roaring in her ears.

Finally Mindy managed to inhale and exhale a deep breath, then another. But the fright remained in her eyes as the little girl looked at Tory.

"I—I—heard—" Mindy started to hyperventilate.

"Nice and easy, baby. Heard what?"

"Mom-my—cry."

Tory wanted to say the right thing. Her mind went blank. *Oh, Lord, please give me the strength to help her, to soothe her pain.* "Did you have a bad dream?"

Tears welled in Mindy's eyes as she nodded. Tory framed the child's face and tugged her toward her, laying her head on her chest and pressing her close.

"It was only a dream, baby. Not real."

"I—know." Mindy hiccuped. "Still—" A shudder rippled down the child's length.

"It seemed real to you?"

Mindy nodded, her breath catching. "I didn't—" Again the child fought for her next words. "Say—bye."

Tory wrapped her arms tighter about the little girl, wanting to hold her and never let her go. "Did you go to the funeral?"

Mindy shook her head. "In hosp-it—" She didn't finish the word.

"I'm sorry, baby. Have you talked to your dad about this?"

"No." Her muffled reply came out on the end of a sob.

"He should know. Do you want me to talk to him for you?"

Mindy pulled back, tears still shining in her eyes. "Plee-ze."

"Are you sure?"

"I—can't make—him sad."

Mindy's own sadness tore at Tory's composure, leaving it shredded. In that moment she would do anything for the child. Was this how mothers felt about their children? "Then I'll talk to him."

Mindy's stomach rumbled.

"I think a certain little girl is hungry. You did a lot today. Why don't you help me with dinner? When your father comes to pick you up, I'll see if he would like to stay and eat."

Mindy labored to her feet with her good hand reaching out to grasp Tory's. "Good. Dad-dy—doesn't—uh—cook."

"What have you two been eating since Mrs. Watson left?"

"Piz-za—take—" frustration pinched Mindy's features into a frown "—out."

"Well, then tonight you two will have a home-cooked dinner. I pride myself on my cooking skills."

Tory rose and walked with Mindy into the kitchen, a large, cheerful room with plenty of sunlight and floor-to-ceiling windows that overlooked the pasture behind the house. Blue, yellow and orange wildflowers littered the meadow as though a painter's palette had been dumped there. A huge oak tree with a tire swing stood sentinel over the backyard.

"Do you like spaghetti?" Tory asked, going to the sink to wash her hands.

"Yes!" Mindy followed suit and used a paper towel to dry them.

"Then that's what we'll have. I'll chop up the onions while you man the skillet and brown the ground beef."

"I'm—the cook? I've—never."

"You're eight. It's about time you started. I can teach you." The second Tory said the last sentence she realized she might not be able to carry through with her promise. She was assuming more than she should and wished that were different. Since Mindy came into her life, she'd found an added purpose that had been lacking before.

"Wait—till—Dad-dy sees—this." Wearing an apron, Mindy stood on a stool to brown the meat using a wooden spoon and a gloved hot pad.

An hour later the doorbell rang. Tory left Mindy to finish setting the table while she hurried into the entry hall. She opened the screen door to admit

Slade, looking tired but with a smile of greeting on his face. Stepping into the house, he drew in a lungful of air, peppered with the scents of onion, ground beef and baking bread, and licked his lips.

"What do I have to do to wrangle an invitation to dinner out of you?" he asked as he made his way back to the kitchen where Mindy was seated at the large oak table in front of the bay window.

"I—picked—these." Mindy pointed to a glass vase full of multicolored wildflowers from the meadow behind the house.

"Does this mean we are staying?" Slade asked, eagerness replacing the lines of exhaustion on his face.

"Unless you have somewhere else you need to be." Tory removed the loaf of French bread from the oven and placed it in the center of the table. "Mindy didn't think you would mind since you're probably sick of take-out."

Slade walked to the stove and peered into the large pot of simmering spaghetti sauce. "I must have done something right today. This smells divine."

"You'd probably say that about anything you didn't have to fix or order at a fast-food place."

"True. But this exceeds anything I could have imagined."

Heat scored her cheeks. She was always uncomfortable with compliments. "Have a seat next to Mindy," Tory said, and dished up the food.

After placing the bowls on the table, she sat across from Slade and said, "Mindy, do you want to say the prayer?"

The little girl clasped her hands and bowed her head. "Thank—you, Lord, for—" Mindy lifted her head, her brow wrinkled in thought "—for this."

The simple but effective prayer brought a lump to Tory's throat. Every day, Mindy's bravery was a wonderful example to her. The child had to relearn so many things, but not much got her down. Tory was sure the girl's frame of mind was part of the reason for her fast recovery.

After dishing up his food, Slade slid his forkful of spaghetti covered in the thick meat sauce into his mouth. He closed his eyes, a look of contentment on his face. "I can't believe it, but it tastes even better than it smells."

"Mindy was the best little helper I could have."

The eight-year-old straightened her shoulders and announced, "I put—spa—this—in the water." Mindy gestured toward the spaghetti. "Salt—too."

"I didn't realize you could cook, sweetheart. I'll have to get you to fix something for me."

"Real-ly?" Mindy's eyes grew big and round.

"Yeah. Maybe Mrs. Watson will let you help her in the kitchen and teach you some dishes."

"Have you heard from Mrs. Watson?" Tory asked while breaking off a slice of buttered bread from the warm loaf.

"She called last night to tell me her niece and baby boy are doing fine. She'll probably be back by the first of next week. She's going to stay a few days longer than planned."

"Well, if you need me to watch Mindy at the first of next week, that'll be fine with me."

"Yip-pee!" Mindy clapped and bounced in her chair. "We—could—cook—again."

"That would be great," Tory said, her regard resting on Slade, waiting for his answer to her offer.

"How can I say no, especially if I can get another dinner out of it?"

"Are you wrangling for another invitation to dinner?" Tory grinned, responding to the teasing light in his blue eyes.

"You're a sharp lady."

"I have my moments. What do you like to eat?"

"Anything that doesn't move."

"My, that leaves the door wide-open. Are you sure you don't want to narrow it down some?"

"I'll put myself in you two ladies' hands. After all, you're doing me a favor so I can't be too demanding."

The word *demanding* sent a chill down Tory's spine. She clenched her fork and dropped her gaze to her half-empty plate. "Mindy and I will come up with something."

"Our—uh—secret," Mindy said with a giggle.

For the next few minutes while everyone finished their dinner, silence dominated the large kitchen except for the ticking of the clock over the desk by the phone. Mindy finished first, dragging the napkin across her face.

"Can I—swing—on the—tire?" the little girl asked Tory.

"Sure, if it's okay with your father."

"I'll walk you out there." Slade rose.

"No, Dad-dy—I can—do it—by my-self." Mindy pushed to her feet and started for the back door.

Slade took a step toward his daughter.

"She'll be all right. She went by herself to pick the flowers for the table. She wanted to surprise you with them."

Slade peered at Tory, worry in his gaze. The door opened and closed, its sound emphasizing Mindy's need for independence.

"I'm letting her do some things alone. It's important to her."

"But she still falls sometimes."

"All children fall. In fact, earlier today she fell in the barn, but she picked herself up and continued with what she was doing."

Slade stared out the large window that afforded him a good view of the oak tree with the tire hanging from it. He watched his daughter wiggle her body through the hole and lie on her stomach. He scrubbed his hands down his face and forced his attention away from Mindy. "Can I help you clean up?"

"I'll get—" Tory saw Slade's need to keep busy and said instead, "Sure. I'll rinse. You put the dishes in the dishwasher."

"I think I can manage that."

While Tory put the leftover food in the refrigerator, Slade cleared the dirty dishes from the table and stacked them beside the sink. A couple of times his gaze strayed toward the window, his mouth pinched in a frown.

"It's hard letting go." Tory turned the water on

to rinse off the worst of the food before handing the dish to Slade.

"Yes. Mindy's been through her share of pain and then some. I don't want her to have to suffer anymore."

"All parents feel that way, but suffering is part of life. In fact, it probably makes us stronger people." At least, that's what I keep telling myself while going through my own ordeal, Tory thought.

"She's eight years old. Enough is enough."

"She's done a wonderful job of bouncing back."

"She still has a ways to go."

"But she will make it. I predict this time next year you won't be able to keep up with her and she'll talk your ear off."

"I look forward to that prediction coming true." Slade closed the door to the dishwasher and leaned back on the counter, his arms folded over his chest. "You really think she's doing okay?"

Tory smiled. "Yes. You should see her with the young riders. I have a class of three-, four- and five-year-olds and she's great with them. Like a pro."

"Speaking of classes, Mindy tells me about how hard you work to keep this operation up and running. You could use some help around here."

"Don't I know it. But that costs money, money I don't have."

"After Mrs. Watson returns and things settle down, I could take a look at your books and see if I can help in any way. Even though I'm not an accountant, I've taken a few classes in order to help me with my business."

Tory lifted her shoulders in a shrug. ''Sure. With the stable, I've learned to accept help where given.'' She wiped down the sink, then draped the washcloth over the edge. ''I told Mindy I would talk to you about something that happened earlier today.''

''This doesn't sound good.''

''She had a bad dream this afternoon while she was taking a nap. She told me she remembers her mother crying the last time she saw her.''

Tension whipped down Slade's length, his expression unreadable.

''She said she didn't get to go to the funeral for her mother.''

''She was still in the hospital.'' The defensive tone in Slade's voice spoke of the emotions he was holding in check.

''She didn't get to say goodbye to her mother and I think that's bothering her.''

His eyes became diamond hard and his jaw clenched.

Tory cleared her throat, its dryness making it difficult to speak. ''I thought I would take her to her mother's grave site and let her say goodbye, unless you would like to. I think she needs to for closure.''

A nerve in his cheek twitched. He walked toward the window that overlooked the backyard. ''No. I will when everything settles down with Mrs. Watson.''

''I'll go with you, if you want.''

''I—'' Glancing outside, Slade went rigid, then spun toward the door and yanked it open.

Chapter Three

Slade rushed out the back door toward Mindy who lay on the ground by the tire swing. Tory quickly followed. As he approached, his daughter pushed herself to her knees and struggled to stand. All he saw was the scraped skin on her shin and blood beading around the wound. The heaviness in his chest made his breaths shorten.

He scooped up Mindy into his arms. ''Are you all right, baby?''

She squirmed. ''Dad-dy—oo-kay.''

Slade started for the house.

''No! Swing!'' Mindy continued to wiggle until he put her down. She headed for the tire.

''But your leg—''

Tory touched his arm, stopping his progress toward his daughter. ''She'll be fine. I'll take care of the scrape later.''

He swung his attention from his daughter to the petite woman who stood a foot from him. The physical contact was so brief that Slade wondered if Tory's fingers had grazed him. Now her hands were laced together so tightly that her knuckles were white and tension lined her features.

"Why don't you push her while I go get a Band-Aid and something to clean up her shin?"

Slade watched the woman, who had been a part of his daughter's life for months, who was becoming very important to Mindy. Tory walked toward the back door with a grace and confidence Slade had seen when she dealt with her horses. But beneath that layer of assurance was a vulnerability that drew him to her. She had been so good with Mindy. He wanted to help her as she had helped him. But he didn't know what the problem was.

"Dad-dy."

He twisted toward Mindy. "Do you want me to push you?"

"Yes!" Mindy began to worm her way through the hole in the tire.

Slade grasped her around the waist and situated her safely on the swing with her arms looped around the rubber and her legs dangling in front. He gripped the tire and brought it back a few feet, then let go. His daughter's squeals of laughter erased his earlier concerns. In the past twenty-two months he hadn't heard that sound nearly enough. Tory was not only good *with* Mindy but *for* her, as well.

The back door slamming shut indicated Tory's return. Slade peered over his shoulder as she approached him, noting the shadows of dusk settling over the yard, obscuring her expression. He gave his daughter a few more pushes, then let the swing come to a slow stop.

"I hate to cut this evening short, Mindy, but it's getting late and we have to get up early tomorrow and come back out here."

Mindy squirmed through the hole, resisting any help from him. She stood patiently while Tory dabbed some hydrogen peroxide on the scrape, then covered it with a Band-Aid.

Tory straightened. "Why don't you let Mindy spend the night with me? That way she'll get to bed on time and you won't have to drive all the way back out here tomorrow morning."

"Yes!" Mindy clapped her hands. "Plee-ze."

"She doesn't have her pajamas or toothbrush."

"I have a T-shirt she can wear and I have an extra toothbrush. She can wear the extra clothes she has out here and you can bring another set tomorrow evening."

Slade took in his daughter's eager face and said, "Okay, if you're sure."

"I wouldn't have asked if I wasn't."

"Goo-dy." Mindy started for the tire swing.

"No, young lady. You need to get ready for bed."

His daughter's lips puckered into a pout. "But—Dad—"

"Mindy, your father's right. We'll need to get up early to take care of the horses."

"Oh yeah." Mindy's pout disappeared as she began her trek toward the house without another thought to the tire swing.

"I don't think I've ever gotten that quick of a turnaround about bedtime."

Tory grinned. "It's all in what you can offer them."

"And you have the advantage. You've given her something to look forward to. Thank you."

"It's been my pleasure."

Two red patches graced Tory's cheeks, heightening her quiet beauty. She veiled the expression in her large brown eyes and started to follow Mindy into the house. The woman's every motion was economical, nothing wasted, Slade thought as he observed her mount the steps to her deck. He inhaled deeply of the spring air, laden with the scent of wildflowers and earth. Scanning the backyard surrounded by fenced pastures, he decided that he liked the country and its seemingly slower pace.

"Again, thank you for letting Mindy stay over. I hope she goes to sleep. She was so excited when I said good-night." Slade stepped out onto the front porch.

Tory came out, closing the screen door but leaving the wooden one open. "I'll check on her in a few minutes and see if she fell asleep."

"Don't let her talk you into staying up. She's quite good at that."

"Then she's met her match." Tory leaned into the wooden railing and scanned the darkness that blanketed the landscape. A firefly flew near. She observed its progression across her yard and into the trees that lined the west side of her house. When the blackness swallowed up the insect, reminding her of the lateness of the hour, her tension grew at the isolation and night surrounding them.

"You do have a way with Mindy. You're a natural with children."

The compliment washed over Tory, easing some of the distress trying to weave its way through her. "I love children. That's one of the reasons I started the riding program."

"You'll be a wonderful mother someday."

This compliment bore a hole into her heart, and she felt as though the rupture bled. She didn't see herself having children anytime soon, and yet according to her doctor, her time was running out. An uncomfortable silence fell between them, one that compelled Tory to say, "In order to be a mother you have to have a husband. I don't see that happening."

Slade tilted his head and stared at her. "Why not? You're an attractive, intelligent woman." The intensity in his eyes pierced through the layers of her reserve.

"My life revolves around my stable and my work" was the only answer she could find.

"The right man could change that."

"And disappoint all the children?" Her voice husky, Tory shook her head. "I don't think so."

He chuckled. "I guess I shouldn't argue with that. After all, my daughter is benefiting from your work and the Bright Star Stables." He reached out and squeezed her hand. "I'd better be going. Long day tomorrow."

Even though his casual touch lasted only a second,

an eternity passed while Tory fought for her composure. The feel of his fingers around hers had burned into her skin. It had taken all her willpower not to yank her hand from his and flee into the house.

''Good night,'' she murmured as he left. Trembling, she brought her arms behind her back and laced her fingers together.

For a short time tonight she had glimpsed what it would be like to have a family. The yearning had blossomed in her heart. Then her fears returned and latched on to her, making any thoughts of having her own children an impossibility.

The children's giggles danced on the light breeze. Eyes closed, Tory threw back her head and let the sunlight bathe her face in warmth. The gentle lapping of the water against the shore and the serenade of a mockingbird nearby mingled with the continual laughter from Mindy and her best friend.

After spending the morning at church, this was a perfect way to spend the afternoon, Tory thought, opening her eyes to her bright surroundings by the pond. A family of geese swam from the other side toward the little girls who tossed bread crumbs on the ground by their feet.

''I'm glad Mindy's friend could come,'' Tory said, shifting on the blanket spread over the thick, lush grass by the water.

''So am I. She hasn't gotten to see Laurie much this past year. Thank you for making the suggestion that Mindy bring a friend.'' Slade sat by a tree.

With her arms propping her up, Tory leaned back,

watching the children with the geese all around their feet. "Being with friends can be an important part of the healing process."

"And I've isolated her too much?"

Tory peered at Slade with his back against the large oak tree, one leg drawn up with his arm resting on it. The vulnerability in his voice matched the look in his eyes. "She's been pretty busy this past year recovering from the operation and the accident."

"Now it's time to move on?"

"Yes. She told me the other day she wants to go back to school in the fall. She misses her friends."

Slade flexed his hand, then curled his fingers into a tight fist.

"What are you waiting for? For everything to be perfect? That's a tall order. When is any situation perfect?" Tory knew she was pushing, but this was important to Mindy, so therefore important to her.

Slade blinked rapidly several times as though he hadn't realized the implication of his actions for Mindy. "I just don't want her hurt anymore. Last month we went to the mall for some new clothes and a couple of children laughed at Mindy when she walked by. She acted as if she didn't hear them, but there were tears in her eyes. I don't want that to happen to her at school. She'll hate going."

"God only gives us what we can handle."

Slade shoved to his feet, a scowl creeping into his features. "Mindy has handled enough for an eight-year-old."

"She has said something about going to church with me some Sunday. I would love for her to come.

She said she used to go with you and your wife, but not since the accident.'' Tory rose, feeling at a disadvantage with Slade hovering over her. She moved back a few paces into the warmth of the sunshine.

''Things have been so hectic and—'' He paused, inhaled a deep breath and continued. ''No, that's not quite true. I feel God has let my family down. He took away Mindy's mother. He took away who my daughter was. She's had to start over, relearning the simplest things. What kind of God puts a child through that? Why couldn't it have been me?''

The anguish that marked his words settled heavily over her. She needed to soothe his pain away. ''We don't always know why God does what He does, but He has reasons we don't always see at first. What Mindy is going through now will shape the type of person she becomes. That may be a good thing in the long run.''

''So suffering makes a person better?''

''Sometimes. It can open a person up to other possibilities, more life-affirming ones.'' Tory thought of her own change in the direction her life had been heading. Right now she could still be working for that large manufacturing firm in Dallas, never knowing the power of God's healing through animals, never having seen the joy on the children's faces when they rode a horse.

Slade turned his back on Tory and stared at his daughter retreating from the horde of geese demanding more bread, her giggles attesting to her happiness. ''I'm sorry, I don't buy that.''

"Time has a way of changing a person's perspective."

"Not all the time in the world would ever change how I feel about this."

"But fighting what has already happened won't make it go away."

He spun toward her, a frown descending. "I should go with the flow?"

"Accept the changes and make the best of them."

"No!"

The anger in his voice, the slashing scowl, caused Tory to tense and step away from him. Every nerve ending sharpened to full alertness.

His gaze drilled into her for a long moment, myriad emotions flickering deep within. Suddenly his frown collapsed, any anger he had evaporating. He plunged his fingers through his hair once, twice. "I'm sorry. I get so frustrated when I think of all that Mindy has gone through and still has to go through. All I want to do is make things better for her." He rubbed his hands down his face. "It should have been me, not Mindy. Don't you see that? She had nothing to do with the accident. She was an innocent bystander who happened to be sitting in the back seat of the car."

The defeated look in his eyes impaled Tory's heart, reminding her of how much pain had already been suffered by this man and his daughter. She moved toward him, wanting to comfort him. "Were you driving the car?"

His fingers delved into the black thickness of his

hair over and over as though he wasn't sure what to do with his hand. "Yes."

That one word, full of guilt, hung in the air between them. Anguish etched deep lines into his face. Her heart twisted in a huge knot that seemed to lodge in her throat.

"A young man late for an appointment ran a red light. I didn't see..." His husky whisper trailed off into the silence.

"So you blame yourself for the accident. You didn't run the red light. It wasn't your fault."

"But if only I had seen the car in time, I could have done something. By the time I slammed on the brakes and swerved, it was too late." He stared off into the distance as though he were reliving the nightmare all over again, his eyes dull with the memories.

"Sometimes things happen that we have no control over." Control was always the issue, Tory thought, fighting her own sudden tightness about her chest. She struggled for a breath of air. Up until lately she had done so well keeping her own demons at bay. Why now, when she had a new life, must she be reminded of her own past pain?

"I know life can throw us a curve at any moment."

Tory swallowed the lump in her throat and asked, "How will you blaming yourself help Mindy?"

He stabbed her with narrowed eyes. "Don't talk to me about blame until you've walked in my shoes."

Tory dropped her gaze from his unrelenting one,

looking beyond his shoulder toward the pond. She took a moment to gather her frayed composure before saying, "True, I haven't walked in your shoes, but I've done my share of blaming myself when I really had no control over the situation. I've discovered it does no good and doesn't change a thing for the better."

"I need to check on Mindy. I don't want those geese to attack her."

"I think we would have heard—" Tory didn't finish her statement because Slade had left, striding toward his daughter, his arms stiff at his sides, his hands opening and closing.

Tory's muscles released the tension gripping them, and she sank down onto the blanket. Shivering, she drew her legs up and hugged them to her chest while she watched Slade place his hand on Mindy's shoulder and listen to his daughter and Laurie talk about the geese, their voices drifting to Tory. Mindy pointed to one of the adult geese herding the rest of them toward the pond. A baby, trying to scurry to catch up with the group heading back to the water, brought a huge grin to the little girl's face, emphasizing the power animals had over people.

"Hey, is anyone hungry?" Tory called out to the trio by the water.

"Yes," both girls answered.

Slade took Mindy's hand and led the group to the blanket under the tree. "Are you kidding? We've worked up quite an appetite watching those geese gobble up all that bread."

"Oh, Dad-dy—you're—al-ways—hun-gry."

"And I know what a good cook Tory is. I've been saving room for this picnic lunch since she asked us. I could eat a bear."

Mindy put her hand over her mouth and giggled.

"Well, I'm fresh out of bears today, but I have fried chicken. Will that be all right?" Tory asked the group.

The girls nodded while Slade licked his lips, his eyes dancing with merriment.

"Bring it on," he said while settling on the blanket across from Tory.

Mindy sat next to Tory with Laurie on her other side. The picnic basket was in the middle of the circle, every eye on it as Tory slowly opened the lid, releasing tantalizing aromas. She made a production out of delving into the basket and slowly bringing the contents out for everyone's view. Next to the chicken she placed a plate of chocolate-chip cookies, Slade's contribution to the lunch, a bowl of coleslaw and a container of sliced strawberries, pineapple and bananas.

After saying a brief prayer to bless the food, Tory said, "I prefer not to have to take any of this back with us so dig in."

"If we can't finish this off, I volunteer to take the leftovers home with Mindy and me." Slade raised his hand as though he were in school and he was waiting for the teacher to pick him.

"You've got yourself a deal," Tory said, laughing. "But of course, if Mindy and Laurie keep piling it on, there won't be any left for either of us *today,* let alone any leftovers."

Slade tried to sneak a chicken leg from Mindy's plate. She captured his hand and pried it out of his grasp. Then he turned to Laurie who hid her goodies behind her back.

"I think you're gonna have to fend for yourself. It really isn't very hard to fill your plate with food. Here, let me show you." Tory demonstrated how, by putting a piece of chicken on her paper plate, followed by a scoop of coleslaw then fruit salad.

"How about a cookie? Dessert is the most important food here, in my opinion. That's why I volunteered to bring it. I know a bakery that makes the best cookies I've ever eaten." Slade inched his hand toward the plate.

Tory gently tapped him on the knuckles with a plastic spoon. "You're supposed to be setting an example."

Slade grinned. "I thought I was supposed to be eating lunch."

"Is your dad always this ornery?" Tory exaggerated a stern look.

Mindy bent over in laughter.

He quirked a brow. "I don't believe that's a compliment."

"Well, at least you're astute."

"Mindy, come to your dad's defense," Slade said while plucking up the last chicken leg and waving it like a sword.

Mindy and Laurie continued to giggle.

"No help there," he muttered, and dumped the last of the coleslaw onto his plate. When he took a bite of the chicken, he smacked his lips and said, "Mmm. This is better than my mother can fix."

Tory nodded, saying, "Thank you. I'll take that as a compliment."

"Of course," he continued as though she hadn't spoken, "my mother has never fried a chicken in her whole life." He looked innocently at Tory while putting a spoonful of coleslaw into his mouth. "And this is as good as Aunt—"

Tory held up her hand to stop him. "I think I've had enough of your *compliments* for the day."

For the next ten minutes everyone ate their lunch to the sounds of the geese honking across the pond. Mindy craned her neck to see what was going on while cramming a cookie into her mouth, then snatching up another one.

Laurie stood and moved toward the water. "They're chasing away a beaver."

Mindy struggled to her feet. "Bea-ver?"

"There's a family on the other side. They dammed the stream that feeds into the pond and have built their home there."

"Can we go look?" Laurie asked.

"Can we?" Mindy stood next to her friend, observing the commotion across the pond.

"Let me finish eating and I'll go—"

"Dad-dy, I can—go a-lone." Mindy straightened her shoulders and lifted her head.

Slade threw a glance toward Tory, one brow arched in question.

"Stay away from the edge of the pond and stay on the path," Tory said.

When the girls started toward the other side, Slade came to his feet to keep an eye on their progress. "Are you sure they'll be all right?"

"They'll be fine. The path is wide, worn and level."

Slade bent and picked up his paper plate to finish eating his lunch while he observed Mindy. "You probably think I'm being overprotective, but I don't want anything else to happen to my daughter."

"You're doing what you think is right."

"It's the parents' job to protect their children. I let her down once. I won't do it again." Slade popped the last bit of food into his mouth.

"Mindy doesn't feel that way. She thinks you're terrific."

"She talks about me?" Slade dropped his empty plate into the trash bag, then lounged against the tree, his arms folded over his chest, his legs crossed.

"All the time."

Both of his brows rose, his sky-blue eyes growing round. "And?"

"She wishes you didn't have to work all the time."

"So do I, but all her doctor bills and therapy cost a lot of money. I want the very best for Mindy. Hopefully after my company's expansion is complete, I'll have more time for my daughter."

There was so much Tory wanted to say to Slade, but his look didn't encourage further discussion. She didn't have the right to interfere, even if she had come to love Mindy like a daughter. "Have you heard from Mrs. Watson? Will she be back soon?"

A scowl darkened the expression on his face. "No."

"Is there a problem with her niece or the baby?"

"Everyone's fine. The problem is she now wants to stay and take care of her niece's baby. She feels her family has to come first and her niece can't find good arrangements for the baby. I know she's right, but still—" He clamped his mouth closed on the rest of his words.

Tory pushed to her feet. "What are you going to do now?"

Slade stared at his daughter on the other side of the pond, his brows slashing downward. "I don't know. I have to find another housekeeper, which I know won't be easy. I felt so lucky when I found Mrs. Watson."

"I'll be glad to watch Mindy until you get a new one."

"I can't—" He stopped midsentence and looked back at Tory. "Are you sure you don't mind? Because frankly, if you do, I'm not sure what I'm going to do."

"This past week with Mindy has been great. I enjoy the company and she loves working with the animals. She's even taken to the cat and her new litter that lives in the barn."

"No wonder she's been pestering me about getting a cat."

"She's named all the kittens, and after feeding and grooming Mirabelle, that's where she goes next to check up on them."

"I just found out yesterday about Mrs. Watson not

returning. I haven't had a chance to get in touch with the agency yet, but I will first thing tomorrow. I promise I'll get someone as soon as possible. In the meantime, I'll pay you for taking care of Mindy."

She could use the money, but for some reason she couldn't find herself accepting payment for something she wanted to do. Taking care of Mindy was important to her—an act of love. "No. Mindy is giving me as much as I'm giving her."

"But—"

A shout from across the pond snatched the rest of Slade's protest. He whipped about, every line in his body taut.

Chapter Four

Slade sprinted forward. Tory whirled around, her heart thumping against her chest. Mindy had fallen at the edge of the pond and now sat waist-deep in the water. Her scream of surprise turned to giggles as Laurie plopped down beside her and began splashing her.

Slade slowed to a jog. The tension in his body eased. Tory scooped up two kitchen towels she'd brought, the only thing she had to dry off the girls with, and hurried after Slade, thanking God the whole way that the children were all right.

When Slade halted near Mindy, she paused in her water fight with Laurie, looked at her friend, then they both began pelting Slade. The astonishment on his face made Tory laugh. She stood back from the girls, out of their reach, trying to contain her laughter. She couldn't.

Slade stepped back, tossing a glance over his shoulder at Tory. "I'm glad you're enjoying yourself, Miss Alexander.'' Water dripped from his face and hair, soaking his shirt. Beneath his mocked exasperation his eyes danced with amusement.

''Yes, I am.'' Tory brought her hand up to cover her mouth, but her laughter still leaked out.

Slade huffed. ''Melinda Marie Donaldson, you need to get out of that pond right this minute.''

''Oh, Mindy, you're in *big* trouble. Your dad used your full name.'' Laurie stood.

Mindy flung her hand across the water one last time, sending it spewing up toward her father. ''I'm—stuck—Dad-dy.''

While the last spray of water rolled in rivulets down his face, Slade's mocking scowl crumbled into a look of concern. He hurried forward to pick up Mindy.

The little girl held up her hand. ''Help—me—st-and.''

The water lapped over Slade's tennis shoes as he took his daughter's arm and assisted her to her feet. He whispered something into Mindy's ear, then she said something to Laurie.

When they all faced Tory at the side of the pond, soaking wet while she was dry, her laughter died on her lips. ''Okay, what are you all up to?''

''Nothing,'' Slade said, all three of them heading toward Tory with determination in their expressions.

She backed up, her heart beginning to race. The feeling of being cornered suddenly swamped her. ''Stop right there.''

No one did. Sweat popped out on Tory's forehead. Her heartbeat accelerated even more. She continued to step away from the trio while trying to tamp down her fear. But she couldn't control the trembling that shook her body, nor the perspiration rolling down her face. Tory's gaze flitted from the group to the area around her. That was when she realized she was standing at the edge of the pond in some tall weeds, her tennis shoes stuck in the mud.

Slade stopped, putting his arm out to halt Mindy and Laurie. "Girls, she's our ticket back to the barn. We'd better take mercy on her." He clasped Mindy's shoulder. "And speaking of the barn, we need to gather everything up. Laurie has to be home by five and we'll need to take care of our horses before we leave."

"Aw, Dad-dy."

"Scoot." He turned Mindy toward the blanket and prodded her gently forward. When the children were halfway to the blanket and out of earshot, he asked, "Are you all right?"

His questioning probe drilled through Tory's defenses she'd thrown up. The beat of her heart slowed as she brought the gripped towel up to wipe her face. "Other than my shoes caked with mud, yes."

He took a step toward her.

She tensed.

He halted, his gaze softening. "Thank you for inviting us this afternoon."

Tory blinked at the sudden shift in the conversation. Relieved by it, she offered a tentative smile and said, "You're welcome. Maybe Mindy can bring Laurie out some other time to ride with her."

"May I use one of those towels?" He held his hand out to her but didn't move any closer.

She looked down at the towels each crushed into a ball in her hands. A blush heated her cheeks. "Yes." After tossing one to him, she released her death grip on the other one and relaxed her tense muscles.

Slade wiped his face, then slung the towel over his shoulder and started back toward the blanket at a slow pace. Tory pulled her feet from the mud and followed behind him, her shoes making a squishing sound that announced her arrival. The two girls giggled when they saw her.

She put her hands on her waist. "At least I don't look like two drowned rats. Here. Use this to clean up." Grinning, Tory flung the towel toward Mindy, then sank down by the basket to repack it.

She'd overreacted at the edge of the pond. The children and Slade were only trying to include her in their playfulness. Mindy was important to her and Slade was important to the little girl. She would have to learn to relax better around him because if she was truthful with herself, she'd enjoyed herself today. For a brief time she'd experienced again what it must be like to have a family.

"Glad—Dad-dy out—of town." Mindy took a big lick of her chocolate ice cream.

Tory sat next to the little girl on the porch swing, taking her own lick of her single-scoop ice-cream cone. "You are? Why?"

"Miss—you."

Her simple words tugged at Tory's heart, making her eyes glisten. "I missed you, too. I'm glad you got to spend last night with me." She bit into her cone, the crunching sound filling the silence.

Mindy shifted so she could look up at Tory. "Me—too."

"How's Mrs. Davies? You haven't said anything about your new housekeeper."

The little girl pinched her mouth together. "Don't—like."

"How come?"

"Mean." Mindy twisted back around and licked her ice cream, her shoulders hunched, her gaze intent on a spot on the ground.

"Why do you say she's mean?" Her stomach knotted with concern, Tory placed her ice cream cone on the glass table next to the swing.

Mindy wouldn't look at her. She continued to eat her ice cream, her head down, her shoulders scrunched even more as though she were drawing in on herself.

"Mindy?" Tory slid from the swing and knelt in front of the girl. Lifting the child's chin, Tory asked, "What's happened?"

Tears welled in Mindy's eyes. "She—doesn't—like me."

Desperate to keep her voice calm, Tory took the child's napkin and wiped the chocolate from her face. "Why do you say that?"

"She—likes—to—uh—yell." Her tears fell onto her lap. "Told—some—one on—phone—I'm—a cri-crip-pled—uh—re-tard."

Tory pried the ice cream cone from Mindy's trembling fingers and laid it alongside hers on the glass table, then she scooped the child into her arms and held her tight against her. "You aren't, sweetie. You're a precious little girl who I admire and think is remarkable."

"You—do?" Mindy mumbled against Tory's chest.

Tory pulled back and cupped the child's tear-stained face. "You're such a courageous person. Not many people could have done what you've done as well. Look how far you've come in such a short amount of time."

Another tear slipped from Mindy's eye, then another. "I—love—you."

Tory's heart stopped beating for a split second, then began to pound a quick beat against her chest. Her own tears rose and filled her eyes. "I love you, too." She drew the child to her, kissing the top of her head, the apple-fresh scent of Mindy's shampoo permeating the air. "Have you told your father about Mrs. Davies?"

Mindy shook her head.

"He needs to know how you feel."

"She—was—the six-th—one—he—talked to. Hard—to find."

"Still, he needs to know. I can say something to him if you want."

Mindy straightened, knuckling away the tears. "Yes!" She covered her mouth with her hand, her eyes round. "Look." Pointing to the table, she giggled.

Melted chocolate ice cream pooled on the glass surface, nearly blanketing the whole table. Tory laughed, too. "I think we made a mess. I'll go get something to clean it up with."

Tory hurried into the house and unrolled some paper towels, then retrieved a bottle of glass cleaner from under the sink. She started for the porch. The phone ringing halted her steps.

Snatching up the receiver, she said, "Hello."

"Tory, this is Slade. How's it going?"

The warm sound of his deep, baritone voice flowed through her. Trying to ignore the slight racing of her heart, she answered, "Fine. Are you back?"

"Yes. I thought I would pick up some pizzas for dinner. What do you think?"

"Pizzas as in plural?"

"Yep. Since we all like different kinds."

The implication of his words struck her. Over the past month she and Slade had gotten to know each other well—their likes and dislikes. She was even able to relax around him. "Sure. Mindy will be glad you're home early."

"Tell her I'll be there in thirty minutes."

When Tory hung up, her hand lingered on the receiver. When had Slade Donaldson become such a good friend? The question took her by surprise. Their relationship had changed quickly, something that further surprised her. She hadn't let someone get this close, this fast, in a long time. She knew they both loved and cared for Mindy, but there was something else about their time together that went beyond the little girl.

When Tory returned to the front porch, she found Mindy standing by the rail, staring down at the flower bed. Tory put down the glass cleaner and towels on the swing and came up beside the child.

Mindy angled her head, glancing up at Tory. "Something—big—went—under—house. Uh—dark." The child waved her hand toward the area behind a large azalea bush that had just lost its last red bloom. "What—is it?"

"It's not the cat?" Tory bent over the rail to glimpse into a black hole that led to the crawl space under the house.

"No-oo."

Straightening, Tory shook her head. "I don't know, then. Maybe a raccoon. Two summers ago I had a family move in under the house."

"With—bab-ies?"

"Yep."

Mindy tried to stretch over the railing to get a better look. Tory had to hold her and pull her back when she nearly tumbled into the bush below.

"I want—to see." Mindy pouted, tiny lines crinkling her brow.

"Not right now. Maybe some other time. Your dad is on his way with dinner and we have a mess to clean up."

"He is?"

"He's bringing us pizza."

Mindy's whole face brightened with a big grin. She moved toward the table, her foot dragging behind her more than usual, an indication the child was tired.

"Maybe you should rest before he comes," Tory said while sopping up the melted ice cream with the paper towels.

Mindy grabbed the glass cleaner and sprayed it on the table. "I'm—oo-kay."

The way the child held her left hand curled against her body told Tory otherwise. "Sit. I'll see to this."

Mindy fought a yawn. "Dad-dy—will be—here."

"He still has twenty minutes."

The child backed up against the swing and eased down onto its yellow cushion. She masked a big yawn while leaning back to rest her head. Her eyelids drooped, then snapped open. Tory finished cleaning the table, and by the time she gathered up the dirty paper towels to take back into the house, Mindy's eyes were closed and her head was cocked to the side.

Tory moved the child so she lay on the cushion. Brushing back Mindy's dark brown hair from her face, Tory stared at the little girl who had become so important to her. The child had gotten up with her at dawn to help her take care of the horses and she hadn't stopped the whole day. She'd been by her side while she'd cleaned out the stalls and fed the horses. She'd ridden with her and helped her fix lunch. Mindy filled her life with a renewed purpose.

She'd missed Mindy this past week when Mrs. Davies had started to work for Slade. She'd only seen her when she had her two lessons. When Slade had asked her if Mindy could spend the night since Mrs. Davies couldn't stay with her, she had jumped at the chance to have the girl with her for a full twenty-four hours. It had seemed like Christmas in June.

One of Mindy's legs began to slip off the swing. Tory caught it and tucked it back under her. The child stirred but continued to sleep.

Again Tory brushed a stray strand of hair that had fallen forward behind Mindy's ear. "I wish I was your mother," she whispered. Tears crammed her throat. She wasn't Mindy's mother, would never be. The thought pierced her heart like a red-hot poker.

Slade pulled up in front of Tory's small, one-story white house surrounded by large oaks and maples and felt as though he had come home. Tory rose from a white wicker chair on the porch and waved. Peace rippled through him. Clasping the steering wheel, he closed his eyes for a few seconds to relish that feeling. He could imagine her fragrance of lilacs, the light in her eyes when she smiled, and he held on to that serenity for a couple of seconds longer. Then reality blanketed him in a heavy cloak of guilt. Exhaustion cleaved to him, sharpening the sensation there wasn't enough time in a day to correct what had happened to his daughter.

The aroma of the pizza wafted to him, reminding him that he'd brought dinner and he was hungry. Sliding from the car, he grabbed the three boxes and headed for the porch.

Tory's eyes lit with that sparkle that always made him feel special. He responded with his own grin, saying, "I hope you two are hungry. I got medium ones for everyone."

‘‘Medium! Who else is coming?’’ Tory stepped to the swing and nudged his daughter who lay curled on the yellow cushion, sleeping.

Mindy’s eyes blinked open. She rubbed them as she propped herself up. ‘‘Dad-dy!’’

She started to get to her feet, but Slade motioned for her to remain sitting. He brought her pizza box to her and opened it on the seat next to her.

‘‘Why don’t we eat out here? I’ll go get some lemonade for us to drink.’’ Tory rushed inside, the screen door banging closed.

Mindy stared at her pizza but didn’t pick up a piece.

‘‘Aren’t you gonna dig in? I thought half of it would be gone by now.’’ Slade sat in a chair across from his daughter.

‘‘Can’t. Wait—for Tor-ee. We always—say a—’’ Mindy squinted ‘‘—prayer be-fore eat-ing.’’

‘‘Oh, right,’’ he murmured, remembering a time when he, Carol and Mindy used to do that—before the accident, before his world had been turned upside down and inside out. ‘‘How was your day?’’

‘‘The—best!’’ His daughter’s expression came alive. ‘‘I—helped. I got—to—ride.’’

‘‘You’re becoming quite the rider.’’

Mindy straightened her shoulders, her chin tilting at a proud angle. ‘‘Yep.’’

Tory pushed the screen door open with her foot. Slade rose and quickly took the pitcher of lemonade from her. After the drinks were served, she sat in the chair next to Slade’s, across from Mindy.

"We—wait-ed," Mindy said, carefully putting her glass on the table next to the swing.

Tory bowed her head with Mindy following suit. Slade stared at them for a few seconds, then lowered his. The words of the simple prayer weaved their way through his mind. Had he given up on God too soon? Had he been wrong to stop going to church, to keep Mindy at home? Tory seemed to draw comfort from the Lord. But then she hadn't been responsible for her child struggling each day—

"Dad-dy!"

Mindy's voice penetrated his thoughts. He looked up to find both of them were staring at him as though he were an alien from outer space. His daughter had a piece of pizza in her hand, one bite taken from its end. Tory had nothing. Then he realized he still held the other two boxes in his lap. He quickly passed Tory's to her and opened his own.

"I'll share if you're that hungry," Tory said in a teasing tone.

"Even though I forgot to eat lunch, that one is all yours. The least I can do is provide dinner for you after you watched Mindy for me."

"Looks like I got the better end of the deal. You shouldn't work so hard that you forget to eat."

"Had a flight to catch and a gal to get back to. A mighty pretty gal if I do say so myself." His gaze strayed to his daughter.

Mindy giggled, her mouth stuffed with food. She started to say, "Da—"

"Nope. No words from the peanut gallery, especially when a certain pretty gal's mouth is still full of pizza."

Giggling some more, Mindy covered her mouth.

Tory watched the exchange between father and daughter, the love deep in their eyes. Mindy washed her food down with a big gulp of lemonade.

Slade leaned over and handed his daughter a napkin, pointing to her chin. "You have a red beard."

Father and daughter's shared laughter pricked Tory with longing. She wanted that with a child. She wanted a family. And time was running out for her. She didn't see any way she was going to accomplish that goal. Too many obstacles.

"Was your business trip successful?" Tory settled back in her chair, her stomach knotted.

Picking up his pizza laden with everything but the kitchen sink, Slade said, "Things are proceeding according to my plans. Hopefully I won't have to travel as much in the future."

Mindy clapped. "Goo-dy!"

"I figured you would like that," Slade said, taking a bite of his food.

The little girl popped the last piece of her third slice into her mouth, then took a large swallow of lemonade. Pushing herself to her feet, she said, "Save—for—later?"

"Sure, but I thought you were hungry?" Slade's brow knitted in question.

"My—show—is on." She started for the door.

"Show? What show?" Slade asked as his daughter banged the screen door closed behind her.

Tory shrugged. ‘‘Beats me. She doesn’t watch much TV when she’s here.’’

‘‘She’s always been a fast eater, but she beat her record this time.’’

‘‘I think she wanted to leave us alone so I could talk to you.’’

The frown lines deepened as he shifted his blue gaze to her. ‘‘This doesn’t sound good. What happened?’’

Her stomach muscles constricted even more, tension taking a firm grip on her. ‘‘Mindy doesn’t like Mrs. Davies.’’

‘‘Why?’’

‘‘She overheard the woman calling her a crippled retard to someone on the phone. She doesn’t think Mrs. Davies likes her.’’

Anger slashed across his face. He flexed his hands then balled them. ‘‘A crippled retard?’’

Her own indignation stiffened her spine. She remembered the hurt in Mindy’s voice and expression when she had told her earlier and wanted to demand Slade do something about it.

He tossed the pizza box he held onto the swing and surged to his feet. Every line in his body spoke of his rage. ‘‘She came highly recommended. Her references were excellent. How can—?’’ He paused, opening and closing his hands again, took a deep breath and continued. ‘‘How can anyone say that?’’

‘‘I don’t know,’’ Tory said, having a hard time herself understanding why Mrs. Davies would say that about Mindy, even if the woman didn’t know the child was listening.

Slade scrubbed his hands down his face, then plopped down onto the swing, facing Tory. ''What do I do now? I can't have someone like her taking care of Mindy, but I need someone to watch my daughter. Mrs. Davies was the best applicant from the batch I had. I—'' He snapped his mouth closed and stared at a place behind Tory. When he reestablished eye contact with her, a bleak look was in his expression.

Tory resisted the urge to toss the pizza box to the floor and slip into the place next to him on the swing, taking his hands within hers. It was tempting, but she sat frozen in her chair, watching a play of emotions flit across his features.

A hopeful gleam appeared in his blue eyes. ''Unless you'd like to take the job.''

For a moment Tory forgot about her ranch and the horses, her dream, and thought about accepting the offer, turning her back on the past four years. She loved Mindy and didn't want someone else looking after her. But she couldn't walk away from her dream and the people who depended on her, Mindy being one of them. ''I've grown to love your daughter. I'd be glad to have Mindy come out here, but that's a short-term solution. We could do that until you find someone else.''

''But you're perfect for Mindy. She's always talking about you. She's so comfortable at your place. Isn't there a way we could work this out?''

''It doesn't seem practical.'' Regret tinged her voice. She thought of the long hours she had to spend taking care of the ranch as it was right now. She could manage to help for a while, but without assistance with the ranch, everything would catch up with her. She could only do so much. "There's so much I have to do around here. Going back and forth to town would be very time-consuming."

"What if I moved out here?"

Surprise widened her eyes. "Where?"

He shrugged. "Here?"

"Here!" Her mouth went dry and perspiration cloaked her forehead.

"Yes." Slade rose. "There's got to be something that could work." He began to pace as though he needed to keep moving in order to gather momentum. "Maybe we could get married? For Mindy." The second he said those words, he halted, his eyes huge with shock.

"Married?" Stunned, Tory watched him begin walking again from the swing to one end of the porch, then back.

Chapter Five

"Yes, married," Slade said, moving toward her. He came to sit across from her, pulling his chair closer so that his knees were only inches from hers, the shock replaced with enthusiasm. "I could help you with this ranch. You could hire someone to assist you. You've been worried about money. With my expansion nearly completed, my company's going to be doing well. Money won't be a problem. We could help each other."

Still stunned, Tory listened to his words as though she were a bystander observing the scene from above. She had a hard time getting past the word *married.* "But—" Nothing else came to mind.

"Don't answer me right now. Think about it. We're friends. We both care for Mindy. You would be a terrific mother for her. In fact, I can't think of anyone better for that role. Mindy needs someone like you in her life on a permanent basis. This could be a good partnership.'' The eagerness in his voice made his words rush together.

Marriage? Partnership? Was that a possibility? She'd given up hope of ever getting married, even though she wasn't quite thirty. She'd given up hope of ever trusting enough to have a real marriage. Desperate, Tory grasped on to a sane rational reason not to go through with his proposal. ''Marriage is a serious step. There're so many things involved.''

Leaning forward, he clasped her hands. ''I know. That's why I don't want you to give me an answer right away. Think about it.''

''You should, too.'' The intensity in his gaze burned heat into her cheeks. ''I mean we aren't in l—'' She couldn't seem to say the word. It lumped together in her throat and refused to come out.

''We aren't in love?'' One brow quirked. ''No, but we are good friends. I can tell you things I haven't told another. I trust you one hundred percent with my daughter.''

The last sentence produced a surge of pride. For a moment she relished that feeling, but then reality took over, bringing her back to the problem at hand. ''But what if you find someone later who you fall in love with and want to marry? To me, marriage is forever.''

A shadow crossed over his face, darkening his eyes as if a storm gathered in them. He pulled away and stood. ''I won't. I had that once in my life.'' He paused, angled his head and asked, ''But have you?''

Tension constricted her muscles until she had to force herself to relax. The drill of his gaze prodded her to answer by shaking her head. She didn't think she could ever trust someone that completely that she could let down her guard and fall in love. To be in love was to give more of herself than she thought possible.

"Then perhaps you'll fall in love one day and want to marry?"

She came to her feet, face-to-face with him, only a yard separating them. "No, I won't."

"Why not? You have so much to offer any man."

But not you, came unbidden into her mind, and she wondered why her heart contracted with that thought. She knew she needed to say something, but what? Silence stretched between them; the only sound drifting to her was from the people talking on the television show Mindy was watching.

Slade took one step closer. "Why not, Tory? You're a warm, generous person. You would be a perfect mother. I've seen you with Mindy and the other children you work with."

She wanted to back away, but the chair was behind her. For a few seconds she felt trapped, her heart quickening its pace, her breathing becoming shallow. No, this is Slade. A friend. Mindy's father. Someone she'd been alone with many times. She forced deep breaths into her lungs and said, "I was badly hurt once."

"What happened?"

The question, spoken low, the words laced with compassion, focused all of Tory's attention on the man before her. Painful memories, buried deep, threatened to swamp her. She shoved them back into the dark recesses of her mind, where she was determined they would remain. "Not important now."

He covered the small space between them and took her hands. "I'm a good listener."

The warm, comforting wrap of his fingers about hers attested to the man she had come to know, a man who loved his daughter so much he would marry Tory to give Mindy a mother. "I know."

"When you're ready, I'll be here for you."

His quiet statement mesmerized her. She found herself leaning closer, the scent of his lime aftershave enveloping her in a protective cocoon. He released one hand and cupped her face. She stared into the blue depths of his eyes, no longer stormy but gleaming like diamonds on water. She felt herself become lost, drawn toward his kindness. Was it possible to be more than friends? The honking sound of a flock of geese flying overhead broke Tory's trance.

She pulled back and to the side, forcing a smile to her dry lips. "I appreciate your offer, but to me what has happened in the past is best left in the past." When several feet separated them, Tory turned toward him.

Slade picked up the boxes of pizza. "I'd better get Mindy home. I need to call Mrs. Davies and tell her I no longer need her services."

"Bring Mindy out here tomorrow morning. I'd love to watch her until—"

"Until you decide about my proposal?"

She nodded. "Or, you find someone to take care of Mindy."

His gaze linked with hers. "I've already found someone."

* * *

Moonlight streamed through the window in the living room and pooled on the floor near Tory's feet. Darkness cloaking her, she stared at the circle of light as though there was an answer to Slade's question written in it. But for hours she had fought the demons of her past and still she was no closer to an answer now than she was when she had tried to go to sleep at midnight.

Silence surrounded her. Usually she liked the quiet that reminded her she was alone. But not this evening. She wanted the silence to be filled with the laughter of children, with the voices of daughters and sons. Slade had dangled a dream in front of her—to be a mother. And she couldn't think of a more beautiful child to be her daughter than Mindy.

Pushing herself to her feet, Tory navigated around the coffee table and headed for the kitchen. She flipped on the overhead light and brightness flooded the room, causing her to blink. She put a pot of water on to boil, then sat at the table and waited.

Should she risk marriage to Slade to fulfill her dream? She folded her hands together and bowed her head. *Dear Heavenly Father, please help me make the right decision. There's a part of me that thinks this is the right thing to do. But then my fear takes over and I don't know what to do anymore. I care for Slade. He's a good man. And I love Mindy like she is my own child. Please give me a sign showing me the way.*

A high-pitch whistle disturbed the quiet, startling

Tory. She leaped to her feet and hurried to the stove to remove the kettle. After fixing herself a cup of herbal tea, she sat again at the table, her elbows resting on its wooden top.

What to do? The second hand on the wall clock sounded—tick, tick, tick. Seconds merged into minutes and still no answer.

Nibbling at the back of her mind was the one thing that was stopping her. Being a true wife in every sense for Slade. Could she do that? They hadn't discussed that part of a marriage, but she wasn't naive. She knew he was a man in every sense of the word and would want more from her than she might ever be able to give.

With her eyes closed, she sipped at her tea and tried to imagine life as Slade's wife, as Mindy's mother. The child's laughter, her smile, filled Tory's mind. Mindy's need for a mother sliced through her defenses, urging her to take the risk and deal with the consequences later. If only she could—

Slade prowled his dimly lit den, too restless even to sit. Beyond the picture window he saw that night had lightened to a dark gray. Soon dawn would color the eastern sky with oranges and pinks. Soon his daughter would be up and ready to go to Tory's for the day, eager to spend time with the woman she had grown to love like a mother over the past few months. Soon he would see Tory again.

What would she tell him today?

That question had plagued him all night to the

point he hadn't been able to sleep. One part of him was so stunned he had asked Tory to marry him, but the other felt as though it was the answer to all his problems and the best thing for his daughter. And he would do anything for his daughter. The most important was righting what his child had gone through these past couple of years, giving her back as normal a life as possible.

He could still see the flash of red out of the corner of his eye as the truck ran the light. He could still hear the crunch of metal as the pickup plowed into the passenger's side of his car where his wife sat. And he could still hear his daughter's screams and his wife's moans—the last sounds she made before slipping away. There were times when he imagined the scent of blood and gasoline still hung in the air and the wail of sirens shrieked closer.

If only— He buried his face in his hands and tried to block the images from his mind. He wanted to leave the past in the past as Tory had. But every time he looked at Mindy he was reminded that he had survived with only a few bruises and cuts while his family had suffered.

What had Mindy done to deserve this kind of punishment? What had he done? All he had ever wanted was to love and protect his family. He had failed his daughter once. He wasn't going to again. Tory was the best thing for Mindy, and he was determined to persuade her to marry him and give his daughter the family she deserved.

Standing at the fence watching a mother and colt frolicking in the pasture left of the barn, Tory heard the sound of a car approaching on the gravel road that led to her house. She didn't have to glance over her shoulder to know it was Mindy and Slade. She cradled the cup of tea and brought it to her lips, taking several sips of the now-lukewarm brew. Coldness cloaked her even though the temperature was quickly rising into the mid-seventies. Her eyes stung from lack of sleep, but her jittery nerves kept her moving.

A car door slammed shut, then another one. Mindy called out to her. Tory turned and leaned back against the wooden fence, waving at the little girl as she headed into the barn to see Mirabelle. Dressed in dark blue dress slacks, Slade strode toward her, tired lines marking his features. He hadn't slept much the night before, either. Good, she thought, since his surprise proposal certainly had robbed her of any rest.

Finishing her tea, she placed the mug on the post, more brown than the white it was supposed to be. "When will you be picking Mindy up?"

"I have a late-afternoon meeting with a contractor about the additions to the plant. When I'm through with him, I'll come straight here. It should be by six."

"Mindy and I can have dinner ready for you."

A smile curved his mouth. "I'd like that." He started to say something else but stopped before the first word was out.

"I don't have an answer, if that's what you want to know."

"I figured as much. Did you get any sleep last night?"

She gestured toward her face, sure the circles under her eyes were still evident. "What do you think?"

"No. Neither did I."

"So, I should probably have an answer soon if either one of us wants to get any sleep?"

"Yep, that about sums it up."

His crooked grin melted any defenses she had automatically erected. She pushed away from the post and rolled her shoulders. "I'm not as young as I used to be. There was a time I could stay up all night and keep going strong the next day. That's not the case anymore. I'm hoping Mindy will want to take a nap later this afternoon."

"Since she was up bright and early this morning, I'd say she probably will. She was so excited to be coming out here and not having to stay with Mrs. Davies."

"I'm glad." She started past Slade, making her way toward the barn. "Why don't you let her spend the night? Bring some clothes for her this evening, and when she goes to sleep, you and I can have a talk." She hadn't realized until the words were out of her mouth that she would give Slade an answer that evening. But she would. Now she just had to figure out what that answer would be.

"Then I'll swing by the house and pick up some of Mindy's clothes." Slade stopped at his car and opened the door, throwing Tory a heart-stopping look.

From the entrance into the barn Tory watched

Mindy's father drive away, her time running out. Twelve hours to go.

"Tor-ee, can—I ride?"

She turned toward the little girl standing in the middle of the barn. "Sure, just as soon as I finish mucking out two stalls."

"I'll—help."

"I was counting on that." Tory approached Mindy and clasped her on the shoulder.

The little girl threw her arms around Tory's waist. "I'm—so glad—no—Mrs. Davies. Thank—you."

"You're welcome." Tory leaned back, staring down at Mindy. This child was the reason the answer wasn't a simple no.

"I'm—a good—uh—helper." Mindy puffed out her chest. "You—need—help."

"I tell you what. I need to feed the cat and her kittens. Can you do that for me while I take care of the last two stalls?"

"Sure." Mindy's blue eyes gleamed, big and round.

"You know where their food is?"

The girl nodded.

"I'll come get you then when I'm through."

Mindy started for the tack room while Tory hurried toward the last stall on the left. Twenty minutes later, her muscles shaking with fatigue, Tory went in search of Mindy. She heard the child before she saw her. Mindy was outside the back entrance, talking to the kittens.

She held one in her lap, stroking it and saying, "Maybe—I'll—get to—stay—here. I see—you—

every—day. Wouldn't—that be—nice?'' The child buried her face in the kitten's fur, rubbing it back and forth across her cheek. ''Tor-ee—needs—me.''

Tory's throat jammed with emotions of love. She did need Mindy. More than she realized. Tory closed her eyes for a few seconds. *Thank you, Lord, for showing me the answer.*

Swallowing several times, Tory stepped from the shadows into the light. ''Are you ready to ride, Mindy?''

Dusk blanketed the farm, cooling the air slightly. The dark clouds to the south hinted at a chance of rain. Crickets trilled and frogs croaked. Tory brushed a stray strand of hair, fallen from her ponytail, behind her ear. Taking a deep breath, she relished the scents of grass and earth that mingled with the fragrance of the honeysuckle she'd planted along the fence to the west.

She needed to paint the fences, the barn and the house. Each year more of the white flaked off and yet she neither had the time nor the money to do that. There weren't enough hours in the day.

The screen door banged closed behind her. The sound of even footsteps approached her. She remained by the porch railing, her fingers grasping it a little tighter.

''I finally got Mindy to go to sleep. All she wanted to talk about was the kittens and Belle. She told me when she grows up she wants to work with animals like you, Tory.'' Next to her Slade settled himself back against the railing, his arms folded over his chest, and faced her. "See what kind of influence you have on Mindy?"

She looked away from the intensity in his gaze, warmed by his compliment and a bit afraid she could never live up to what Mindy needed. "It's going to rain tonight. How is Mindy in a thunderstorm?"

"Fine. Unless the thunder gets too loud."

"I love rain. A good storm cleanses the earth."

"So long as it doesn't set in for days at a time."

Tory turned away from the yard and half sat, half leaned on the railing next to Slade, their arms almost touching. "Rain is important to a farmer."

"How long are we going to discuss the weather before we talk about what I asked you last night?"

She slanted a look toward him, her head cocked. "Impatient?"

"Yes, I was patient all the way through that delicious dinner. How did you know I love pot roast?"

"Mindy mentioned it to me."

"I guess I'm a meat-and-potatoes kind of guy."

She suspected he was as nervous as she was about their impending discussion. "Also, according to your daughter, a dessert kind of guy, too."

"Is that why we had blackberry cobbler?"

"Yes."

"Did you and Mindy make that today?"

"Yes, but the ice cream was store-bought. I only have so much time to cook."

"But you enjoy cooking?"

"Yes. I wish I had more time to do that."

"Which brings me to why I am here. I can give

you more time to do those kinds of things. Will you marry me, Tory Alexander?"

The question hovered between them, its implication vibrating the air as though a hundred hummingbird wings beat against each other. She took a deep, fortifying breath and opened her mouth to reply. No words would come out. They lodged in her throat. Swallowing several times, she tried again. "First, we should talk about—" Still she couldn't say what she needed to.

"About what?"

The mere thought flamed her cheeks. She palmed them, feeling the searing heat. "What kind of marriage will we have?"

A dawning light shone in his eyes. "Do you mean, will we have a real marriage in every sense of the word?"

Her heart paused in its frantic beating, then resumed its crash against her chest. Its thundering roar in her ears drowned out all other sounds. Perspiration beaded on her forehead. "Yes," she finally said in a voice stronger than she thought possible.

He shifted so he fully faced her. "I hope so, but, Tory, you will call the shots. It will be up to you."

She veiled her expression. She could accept those terms, but could he? What if she couldn't ever take that step? What if—

No, she would deal with it one day at a time. The Lord would show her the way. She lifted her gaze to his. "Yes, I will marry you."

Tory stood back from the one-story farmhouse and surveyed the freshly painted wood. White with hunter-green trim gleamed in the sunlight, rejuvenating the old structure. Even the swing and wicker furniture on the porch had been painted to match the trim. Turning toward the horse barn, she watched the three painters putting the finishing touches to its hunter-green trim. Then the fences would be painted white. Satisfaction and pride welled up in her.

Eight days ago she had accepted Slade's proposal and the next day he'd had painters out here to discuss painting whatever needed to be done. The following day they'd started and had been working nonstop since then. Slade wanted the work done by the time of their wedding in four days. It would be close.

A blue Honda, at least ten years old, pulled into the drive leading to the house. She waited by the gravel road while the man parked and climbed from his vehicle. Approaching him, she extended her hand. ''You must be Gus Morris.''

The older man with a full head of white hair pumped her arm. ''Yes, ma'am. I sure am. It's a pleasure to meet you.''

''Let's talk while I show you the operation.'' Tory started for the barn.

Gus, who was no more than two inches taller than Tory, fell into step next to her. ''It looks like you're sprucing up the place.''

''Yes.'' Tory gestured for Gus to enter the barn first. ''I have fifteen horses—five of them mine and one pony. I offer classes, usually in the afternoon. The people who stable their horses here come out and ride, some more than others. I make sure the horses are fed and taken care of each day.'' Tory paused in the middle of the barn. ''Also, I keep the stalls clean and keep an eye on the various horses. I'll inform the owner if a problem is developing. As you saw, I have several riding rings and also paddocks and trails for people to use.''

''What will my duties be?''

''Cleaning out the stalls, feeding and watering the horses, keeping the tack in good shape. You'll be assisting me with whatever needs to be done.''

''Hours?''

''From six in the morning until three in the afternoon. You'll have an hour off for lunch.''

The short man grinned, his brown eyes twinkling. ''As I told you over the phone, I miss my ranch. I miss working with horses. My kids wanted me to move here, but they neglected to give me anything to do. I found retirement isn't for me.''

''Do you think you can manage the duties?'' Tory took in Gus's wiry frame.

''Been doing that kind of stuff all my life. Don't you worry about me. I am all muscles, no fat. I'm in good health and driving my daughter bananas. She's actually the one who saw the advertisement in the paper and showed it to me.''

''Then, Mr. Morris, you've got yourself a job and you can start tomorrow if you want.''

''Please, call me Gus. Mr. Morris just makes me seem older than I care to be.''

''Tor-ee—I'm—done.'' Mindy came to the entrance of Belle's stall, holding a curry comb in one hand, hay sticking to her T-shirt.

''Who's this little lady?'' Gus asked.

''This is my helper, Mindy. This is Gus, Mindy. He'll be working here and helping us.''

Gus covered the distance between Mindy and himself in three strides. ''Let me see what you've done.'' He looked inside the stall and whistled. ''That's a mighty fine job, if I do say so myself.''

Mindy beamed. ''Thanks! Belle—is—my—resp—'' Her brow knitted as she glanced toward Tory.

''Responsibility,'' Tory said for her.

''Belle is one lucky pony then.'' Gus turned toward Tory. ''I'll be here tomorrow at six straight up.''

As the old man left, Mindy shut the stall door and made sure the latch was hooked, then she walked toward the tack room to put up her curry comb. ''Dad-dy be here—soon?''

''Soon. But you're staying for dinner again. Your father and I still have to talk about the wedding plans.''

''Four—days. Can't—wait.''

''Ready to help me with dinner?''

Nodding, Mindy took Tory's hand.

''I thought we would have hamburgers tonight. What do you think?''

''Yes.''

When a black Taurus headed toward her house, Tory stopped for a moment, trying to make out who was behind the wheel. Judy? She was early.

''Who's—that?''

"My older sister. She wasn't supposed to come for the wedding until Thursday."

"Sis-ter!" Mindy quickened her pace, nearly falling in her haste.

Tory steadied her. "Slow down. After the day we put in, I don't have that kind of energy. Judy isn't going anywhere."

"Will—she—be my—aunt—when—you—mar-ry—Dad-dy?"

"You bet."

"Neat!"

Judy slid from the car and stretched. "I know I'm early. But Brad told me to come and he'll bring the kids with him in a few days. How can I pass up a minivacation without the children?"

Tory studied her sister's face, her expression innocent, and wondered about Judy's motives behind her early arrival. Her older sister was always trying to protect her. She was sure Judy was here to scout out the situation for Mom and Dad and make a report before they came. "Judy, I want you to meet Mindy. She's Slade's daughter."

Mindy lifted her hand to shake Judy's. "I—help—Tor-ee."

"That's what she said to me. She's lucky to have such a good helper."

Mindy preened, a big grin on her face.

"Pop the trunk and I'll help you with your luggage." Tory moved around to the back of the car. When she saw the jammed trunk, she laughed. "I should have known you'd bring your whole closet with you."

Judy bent down and whispered into Mindy's ear, "Ignore Tory. She likes to make fun of me and what I pack for a trip. My motto is to always be prepared and in order to do that I have to bring choices."

Mindy giggled.

"And of course, Mom had me bring some wedding gifts for you."

"Gifts?" Mindy's eyes grew round. "I'll—help—open?"

"I wouldn't ask anyone but you. Come on, we'd better get started or we'll be out here all night unloading the car."

"Well, Mindy, I think you did a superb job with the baked beans." Judy wiped her mouth on her napkin and laid it on the side of her empty dinner plate. "And the hamburgers were great, Slade. Grilled to perfection."

"Yes—Dad-dy." Mindy finished off her chocolate milk.

Slade pointed to his mouth and waited until his daughter had used her napkin to clean hers before saying, "With compliments like that, I could get used to cooking."

Judy rose and began taking the dishes to the sink. "My contribution to this dinner is to clean up."

"I'll help." Tory stacked several plates on top of each other.

"While you two are doing that, Mindy and I will take a walk down to the barn. I wanted to check out how the painters are coming along."

Tory put the plates into the sink. "If it doesn't rain, I think they'll get finished by the wedding."

When Slade and Mindy left the kitchen, Judy brought a platter and bowl over to the counter. "She's every bit as cute as you said."

"And?"

"What do you mean 'and'?" her sister asked, again that innocent expression on her face.

"I know you, Judy. Is Mom watching the kids so you could come early and pump me for information?"

"Why, Victoria Alexander, I don't know what you're talking about. Brad—"

"You haven't suddenly changed. You're dying to know what in the world has gotten into me. Don't deny it."

Judy placed one fisted hand on her waist. "Okay. I'll admit Mom and I were curious."

Tory barked a laugh. "Merely curious?"

"You weren't even dating anyone the last time I talked to you, what, a week before you made this grand announcement that you were getting married. What's going on?"

"I've known Slade for some time. I don't tell you and Mom everything."

Judy's expression sobered. "Have *you* told Slade everything? Does he know what happened?"

Chapter Six

Tory started rinsing the dishes off to put into the dishwasher, but her hands shook so badly she nearly dropped a plate. Judy reached around her and turned the water off.

"Tory, you can't keep running from the truth."

A band about Tory's chest tautened, constricting the air in her lungs. She drew in a deep breath, then blew it out through pursed lips. Once. Twice. Still she felt as though she were suffocating. Clasping her wet hands together to still their trembling, she closed her eyes, wishing she could block the world out as easily as flipping off a switch. Life wasn't like that. She'd learned that painfully. There were times she felt as though she were running as fast as she could and going nowhere.

She focused on the feel of Judy's arms around her as she said, "The truth? You don't think I've faced it? I have every day for the past four years. As much as I want to forget, I can't. I've tried. Believe me,

I've tried.'' Tears, from the depth of her bruised soul, filled her eyes and coursed down her cheeks.

''Does Slade know about you being raped?''

The question struck Tory with the force of a sledgehammer. Even though she didn't move, she felt as though she had been knocked back against a brick wall. ''No, I don't see why I should share my past with him. It's in my past. It has nothing to do with my future.'' Shame and humiliation nibbled at the edges of her mind. She shut down, refusing them entry.

Judy's arm tightened about Tory. ''Who are you trying to kid? Our past has everything to do with our future.''

Tory wrenched herself from her big sister's embrace and put several feet between them, anger surging to the surface. ''If I tell Slade, it will be when I want to.''

Judy held up her hands. ''I agree, Tory. I won't say a word to him. But that doesn't mean I don't think he has a right to know.''

''Why? Because you think I'm tainted?'' She remembered the looks she'd gotten, the whispers behind her back after she'd brought charges against Brandon Clayton. Cold fingers spread out from her heart to encompass her whole body. She'd felt as if she were the one who had done something wrong, not Brandon.

Horror replaced the concern in her sister's expression. ''No! Never! You know better than to say that. Who held you when you came home that night? Who wept with you? Took you to the hospital? Stood by you through the trial?''

''Why are you doing this now, right before my wedding?''

Judy covered the short distance and clasped Tory's upper arms. ''Because I'm worried about you. Because I want you to be happy. And if that means with Slade, then great. But I know a marriage must be based on the truth.''

''I haven't lied to him.''

''But you aren't telling him everything.''

''I doubt I know everything about him. Who does until they have lived with someone for years, if even then?''

''That's a cop-out, Tory.''

''No, what I'm doing is what I must do to survive.'' Tory yanked away from Judy, sucking in deep breaths of air, her heart pounding against her chest.

''Survive? You—''

The sound of Mindy's and Slade's voices drifted to Tory. The slam of the front door followed by footsteps nearing the kitchen prompted Tory to swipe her hands across her cheeks. She spun about, her back to the entrance while she tried to compose her shattered nerves.

She wasn't the same person she'd been four years ago. She had a right to put that life behind her and move forward. To forget the pain. To grasp on to what happiness she could.

''Tor-ee, I—heard—the ani-mal under—the—house—a-gain.''

Forcing a smile, Tory turned toward Mindy. "You did? She must be making her home there."

"Yep. I—showed—Dad-dy."

The questioning probe of Slade's gaze skimmed over her features. Tory concentrated her attention on the little girl, praying he couldn't see beneath her false facade. "Was everything all right at the barn?"

Mindy nodded. "You—aren't—done?" She glanced at the dishes still stacked at the side of the sink.

"Nope. Judy and I got to catching up and forgot to work."

"I—can—help."

Tory clasped her shoulders, wanting to drag the child against her and hold on to her forever. "You've done enough. I don't want to tire my best worker out."

"Besides, honey, it's time for you and I to get home. The next few days are gonna be plenty busy."

"Dad-dy—do we—have to?" Mindy straightened her slumped shoulders. "I'm—not—tired."

Tory brushed her finger under the child's eye, following the line of a dark circle beginning to form. "Is that so?"

"Well—may-be—a little." Mindy held up her fingers to indicate less than an inch.

"I need you rested. We have to go for our last fitting for our dresses tomorrow."

"Oh—" the child's eyes grew round "—yes!" She grabbed her father's hand and began to tug him toward the door. "We—better—go."

Slade hung back and said over his shoulder,

''Judy, now you see why I think Tory is perfect for Mindy. She works miracles with my daughter. See you tomorrow bright and early.''

When the sound of the front door closing drifted to Tory, she stiffened, curling her hands into tight balls at her sides. The silence of the house eroded her composure. The seconds ticked into a full minute. She knew her sister behind her was trying to decide how best to pursue their earlier topic of conversation.

Tory whirled about. ''I'm through discussing my past, Judy. If you want to stay and enjoy my wedding, then I expect you to respect my decision to put my past behind me and not talk about it. Understood?''

''You've made yourself very clear, but—''

''Don't, Judy. I want you to stay, but I'll ask you to leave if you continue.''

Judy blew out a huff of air, a frown marring her pleasant features. ''Okay, but that won't stop me from worrying about you.''

''I didn't think it would. But I'm a big girl now. I know what I'm doing.''

''Do you?''

No! But with God's help I'll figure it out. Because I have to. For Mindy's sake. For Slade's sake. And most of all, for my own sake.

His wedding ring gleamed in the sunlight. Slade spread his fingers wide and stared at the simple gold band. Married for an hour. He'd never thought he would ever marry again—not after the way his life had fallen apart with Carol's death.

On the light breeze his child's laughter floated to him. He glimpsed his daughter playing with Judy's children, such joy on his child's face. He'd done it for Mindy. He wanted her to have as normal a life as possible. He wanted a mother for her.

Searching the small crowd who'd gathered for his wedding reception, he found Tory talking with her parents and his brother, the only member of his immediate family able to make his wedding since his mother was unable to travel due to poor health. Like flames of a fire, her long, straight auburn hair fell about her shoulders, catching the rays of the sun. The soft folds of her white dress swirled about her knees as she moved with her parents toward her sister and brother-in-law. The tailored bodice and delicate beadwork along the scooped neckline emphasized Tory's petite frame.

She caught him looking at her and smiled. Even across the lawn he saw the sparkle in her gaze as though golden honey mingled with the chocolate of her eyes. Behind that smile there lay a vulnerability that he suspected went deep. It was that very vulnerability that spoke to him and touched his own wounded soul. For a fleeting moment he wondered if it was possible to heal each other's hurts.

He looked away, his gaze dropping to his left hand again. The wedding ring felt heavy and tight. He twisted the band around, a momentary sense of panic attacking. What had he done? He wasn't a whole man. All he could offer Tory was loyalty and friendship. There wasn't anything else left inside.

''It's a little late to be having second thoughts,'' Paul, his friend, said.

''I'm not. This was a good decision. Tory is right for Mindy and me.''

''I have to admit I was surprised by this sudden move. Frankly, I wasn't even aware you were dating.'' Paul peered toward Tory. ''Sandy and I want to have you all over for dinner sometime soon. Maybe after the honeymoon.''

''We aren't going on a honeymoon.''

''Don't let work keep you from going away.''

''You know I'm in the middle of my plant's expansion. I'm putting in a new assembly line to make plastic containers for Wellco. Besides that, I've got several new contracts starting that I need to oversee.'' Slade wouldn't even tell his friend that the real reason he wasn't going on a honeymoon was his marriage wasn't a normal one. Maybe one day, but not now. Paul had already worried enough about him.

''And how does your new wife feel about all this work?''

''She understands.''

''Then you have a special woman because Sandy certainly wouldn't.''

''We'll have a honeymoon later.''

''When that happens, we'd love for Mindy to stay with us. Laurie misses her and all she talks about is that picnic at the pond you all invited her to. She thinks Mindy is one lucky girl to live on a horse ranch.''

''Laurie is welcome to visit anytime,'' Slade said,

realizing he was already beginning to feel the ranch was his home.

That took him by surprise, but as he let his gaze travel over the backyard, the feeling of having come home grew. Already Mindy's toys were evident with a new swing set near the freshly painted white fence separating the yard from the horse pasture. On the deck sat his grill from his house and several blue-and-green pieces of his patio furniture, including a round glass table shaded by an umbrella with big blue flowers on it.

He was selling his house in town even though it was bigger. He had made a commitment to Tory and that involved making her riding stable a success. His home was here now.

''Mom, you should sit down. You've been on your feet too long.'' Tory took a hold of her mother's arm to guide her to the nearest chair. The pale cast to her mother's features worried her. Eleanor Alexander's weak heart had curtailed her activities in the past few years, and today she had overdone it. ''Are you taking your medicine?''

''Yes, dear. I'm just fine.'' Eleanor patted her daughter's arm. ''You worry too much.'' She eased onto the folding chair and indicated Tory sit next to her. ''We haven't had much time to talk these past few days. I never thought you'd be able to put together a wedding so fast, but you did. I wish I could have helped more.''

''You being here is all I need.''

''Well, of course, I'd come to my daughter's wedding, dear.'' A tiny frown furrowed her brow. ''Are you sure, Tory?''

''Now look who's worrying. I'm sure. Slade Donaldson is a good man. I'm lucky to have found him.'' As she said those words to her mother, Tory felt the rightness in every one of them. Slade was an excellent choice for a husband. They were friends. Wasn't that a good reason to marry someone? Much better than passion and love. Ever since her rape, she didn't see her life filled with either of those emotions. When the man she had been dating had forced himself on her, he had taken not only her virginity but her trust in her judgment in men. Slade made her realize not all men were like Brandon Clayton.

Her mother sighed. ''I won't lie to you. I've been worried about you ever since—'' Her mother couldn't voice aloud what had happened to Tory. She never had. Eleanor pinched her lips together, her frown deepening.

Tory laid her hand over her mother's. ''I know. But I'm getting better with each day.'' Some days I don't even think about what happened four years ago. For all her declarations to Slade and Judy about putting the past behind her, she knew in her heart it was always there, just waiting for when she let down her guard. It would have been so much easier if she had lost her memory of the rape. Then she wouldn't wonder if her life would ever be normal again.

''I'm glad, dear. I think this marriage is a good step in the right direction. I like your young man and Mindy is adorable. A ready-made family. I know how important a family is to you.''

And her time for starting her own was running out. Tory had never told her mother that she had been diagnosed with endometriosis. Her mother had been upset enough about the rape. Tory hadn't wanted to add to her mother's worries. She knew how much her mother wanted lots of grandchildren. She'd gotten her love for a large family from her mother.

"Mindy is fitting right in with Ashley and Jamie."

Tory looked toward Mindy playing with her new cousins. "Yes, they hit it off right away. It's nice they are all about the same age."

"Has Judy told you the good news yet?"

"No."

"Oh, dear. I thought she would have told you the first night."

"Told me what, Mom?"

"She's going to have another baby in seven months. But don't say anything. She hasn't told the kids yet. She just found out the day she came up here."

Tory knew the reason her big sister hadn't said anything. She hadn't wanted to put a damper on the festivities. She was happy for Judy and she would let her know as soon as possible. Her sister needed to stop trying to protect her. She'd learned to deal with disappointments, and never having her own children was a very real possibility. "That's great, Mom. Judy probably didn't want to take away from my day."

"Knowing your sister, you're probably right." Her mother peered over Tory's shoulder. "I think Maude is trying to get your attention."

Tory shifted in the chair and found her aunt standing by the long table laden with food. Aunt Maude waved to Tory to come cut the cake she'd baked the happy couple.

Her mother's color still hadn't returned. Her eyes dull, she attempted a smile. ''I think it's time to cut the cake, dear. I'll watch from here.''

''Mom, maybe you should go into the house and lie down.''

''No—'' she fluttered her hand in the air ''—I'm fine, dear.''

''Mother?''

''Go. I see your young man has already been roped by Maude into participating. The groom has to have a bride by his side when he's cutting the cake.''

Tory pushed to her feet, her legs suddenly weak. Her gaze linked with Slade's. For a few seconds the rest of the people faded, and she and Slade were the only two who existed. Earlier that day in her church she'd married him for better or worse, forever. She was now part of Slade and Mindy's family. The implication of what had transpired made her falter as she walked toward her *husband.* Doubts took hold of her heart and squeezed. Had she done the right thing for everyone?

Slade took her trembling hand and clasped it, conveying his support in his gaze and touch. ''Is your mother all right?''

''She says yes, but I think she's overdone it. She'll be the last person to complain if she isn't feeling well.''

''Are you two ready to cut the cake?'' Aunt

Maude asked, snatching the knife off the table and presenting it to Tory.

She grasped it with Slade's hand over hers. The warmth in his palm seared into her. For a second she felt branded, panic swimming toward the surface. She shoved it back down and smiled for the photographer.

Slicing the knife into the bottom layer of the two-tiered carrot cake, her favorite, she prepared the first piece to feed Slade. Her fingers quivered as she lifted the cake to his mouth. His lips closed over the dessert, nipping the tips of her fingers. A tingling awareness chilled her. Dropping her hand away, she entwined her fingers, trying not to shake.

Slade's eyes sparkled like blue fire as he brought her morsel toward her. When she opened her mouth, his finger grazed her bottom lip, again sending a current of sensations zipping through her. She swallowed too soon and nearly choked. Coughing, tears springing to her eyes, she desperately tried to draw air into her lungs and couldn't quite succeed.

Slade patted her on her back. "Tory, are you okay?"

Finally taking a shallow breath, she nodded, unable to speak.

Slade gave her a glass of water that Aunt Maude handed him. Concern etched his features and gave him an endearing appeal.

"It—went down—the wrong way," Tory said.

"When you told me your favorite cake was carrot, I didn't realize you would try to inhale your piece. There will be plenty left for you, I promise."

Tory laughed, all tension fleeing. Slade made her laugh. Slade cared about her. Slade was a loving father. Those were three things she needed to remember as they learned to live together.

''Toast. Toast,'' Brad, her brother-in-law, called out.

Aunt Maude thrust a glass of lemonade into each of their hands.

Slade faced Tory and lifted his high, his gaze connected to hers. ''To a wonderful woman who has opened her home and heart to my family.''

The sweet words washed over her in warming waves. Her mind went blank as she took a sip of her drink. Then it was her turn and still she didn't know how to express her churning emotions. The crowd fell silent, every pair of eyes on her.

She ran her tongue over her dry lips and said, ''To a man any woman would be lucky to have as a husband.''

''Hear, hear,'' someone shouted from the back.

Heat flamed her cheeks as she sipped some more of her lemonade, soothing her parched throat. Tory moved away from the table to allow Aunt Maude and Judy to cut the rest of the cake and pass it out to the guests.

''How are you holding up?'' Slade asked, leaning close to her ear.

His whispered words feathered the nape of her neck and sent a cascade of goose bumps down her spine. She shivered, again a mass of jittery nerves. ''Fine. I will say the past few weeks have been a whirlwind, but the ranch looks nice. And all thanks to you."

"This is my home now. We are partners."

His gaze robbed her of rational thought. She felt lost in the swirling blue depths as though she were drowning in a lake, a whirlpool dragging her under for the third time. "Yes," she managed to say even though her mouth felt dry as an August day in Oklahoma.

"How's Gus working out?"

Tory spied the old man talking to her father and grinned. "He has been a blessing. He may be sixty-eight, but he works like he's years younger. And he knows his way around horses."

"Mindy has taken a liking to him."

"If I'm busy with book work, she's out helping him. He's good with her."

Slade took her hand and brought it up between them, his gaze fastened to hers. "You're good with her."

There was little more than a few inches separating them and Tory should have been afraid. Always before when a man got too close, all her alarm bells rang and sent her flying back. But slowly Slade had insinuated himself into her life until she wasn't scared of his nearness. She even enjoyed his touches. Maybe everything would work out. Hope planted itself in her heart. She wanted her life back. Like Mindy, she was struggling for normalcy.

"Time for you to throw the bouquet."

Her sister's words broke the spell Slade had woven about her. Tory stepped back, her hands dropping away from his. And for a few seconds she felt deprived.

"I've got all the single women lined up below the deck. All you have to do is toss it into the crowd."

"Crowd?" Tory spied the three women by the deck. One was eighteen, another in her thirties and the last in her seventies.

"I can't help it that you know mostly married women. I thought about having Mindy and Ashley join the group, but I don't think either Slade nor I want to deal with two young girls dreaming of getting married just yet."

"You've got that right," Slade said with a chuckle.

"So it's our cousin and two ladies from your church." Judy pushed the bouquet of white roses into Tory's hand.

Tory felt all eyes on her as she strode to the steps that led to the back deck. Perspiration popped out on her forehead. She didn't like being the center of attention, but the day of the wedding the bride always was. She should have eloped. Of course, then her family would never have forgiven her and she suspected Mindy wouldn't have been happy, either. The little girl had been all smiles as she walked down the aisle to the altar earlier that day.

With her back to her guests, Tory tossed the bouquet over her head, then spun about to see Mrs. Seitz nearly shove her eighteen-year-old cousin out of the way to grab the flowers. The seventy-year-old proudly waved the bouquet in the air, catching sight of Mr. Weaver by the punch bowl. He colored a deep red.

After that the guests started to leave, surrounding Tory and Slade to say their goodbyes. Slade by her side felt right. Maybe this could work. *Please, Lord, give me the strength to do what I need to be a good wife and mother.*

The bellow of a bullfrog and the occasional neigh from a horse in the paddock vied with the chorus of insects. The nearly full moon lit the darkness, creating shadows that danced in the warm breeze. Tory, dressed now in shorts and a T-shirt, sat on the porch swing with her legs drawn up and her arms clasping them to her chest. Resting her head on her knees, she listened to the night sounds and thought back over her wedding day.

She was no longer Tory Alexander, but Tory Donaldson. That realization produced a constriction in her chest. She was responsible for more than herself now. Her arms around her legs tightened. Everyone was gone, even her family who were staying at a motel in town and Slade's brother. It was just Mindy, Slade and her. She no longer heard nature's background noise. The lack of voices isolated her, sharpening her senses.

She knew Slade was there before she saw him standing by the steps. She'd heard the soft shuffle of his feet moving across the yard; she'd thought she'd smelled his lime-scented aftershave wafting to her. Lifting her head, she asked, "Did you find it?"

Slade produced the stuffed pony. "By the swing set."

"Good. I know how important favorite toys are."

"I'll be right back." Slade mounted the steps and went into the house.

Minutes later he returned and folded his long length into the chair next to the swing. "She was still awake, waiting for me to bring Belle. After the excitement of today, I'd have thought she would have been asleep the second her head hit the pillow."

"Belle is special to Mindy."

"The stuffed one as well as the real one." He stretched his legs out in front and crossed them at the ankles. "I don't know about you, but when my head hits the pillow, I'll be asleep."

Sleep? She didn't know if she could right now with Slade only a wall away from her. When she had accepted his proposal, she hadn't really thought about the sleeping arrangement. Even though he didn't share her bedroom, they shared a small house. She'd avoided any kind of level of intimacy for so long she wasn't sure how to share one bathroom, the same living quarters, even the kitchen first thing in the morning.

"It has been a long day," she finally said, his silence indicating he expected her to say something. She unfolded her legs and swung them to the floor. Standing, she rolled her shoulders and worked out the kinks.

When he rose, too, the small porch suddenly became smaller. She could definitely smell his after-shave as the scent surrounded her. The distance between them was less than an arm's length. If she wanted, she could reach out and touch him easily. In the dim light from inside the house she could see his handsome features, marked with uncertainty and tenderness.

He quirked a smile. "I realize this is a bit awkward."

"A little." When his smile grew, she said, "Okay, a lot."

He shifted closer, linking his hand with hers. "We'll make this work."

"For Mindy."

"For us, Tory."

His voice, pitched low, flowed over her. She shivered in the warm, June night. His hand slid up her arm, sending a cascade of chills down it. He moved even closer until there was only a breath between them. Cupping her face with his other hand, he stared into her eyes as though trying to read what was in her soul.

Exhausted from the long day and the emotional treadmill she'd been on, Tory melted against him, her legs giving out. He tilted her chin up, pausing for a few seconds before bringing his mouth down on hers. The mating of their lips wasn't like the quick peck at the end of the wedding ceremony; it was a blending of breaths and parrying of tongues. Weak with sensations foreign to her, Tory welcomed the taste of him—until he wound his arms about her, pressing her closer.

Suddenly she couldn't breathe. Panic eroded her composure, prodding her heart to crash against her rib cage. She shoved him away, gasping for air. His startled expression rendered her speechless. She pushed past him, taking the steps two at a time.

The pounding of her bare feet on the cool grass matched the pounding of her pulse. She saw the one light on in the barn and headed for it. Inside she stopped, bending over and drawing gulps of air into her burning lungs.

How in the world had she thought she was ready for this?

What must Slade think? Her husband had kissed her and she had fallen apart. She wrapped her arms around herself and walked toward the back of the barn. Opening the door, she stood staring at the pasture beyond, the moonlight streaming down in a crystal clear sky. The scent of hay and horses saturated the air, a familiar scent that usually comforted her. Except that her heart beat rapidly and she couldn't get a decent breath.

"Tory, what just happened back there?"

Chapter Seven

She tensed, her back to Slade.

"Tory?"

She bit the inside of her mouth, wishing she had an easy answer to his question. Staring at the ribbon of moonlight pooling in the meadow, she whispered, "I'm not ready to take our relationship to the next level."

"Is that what you thought that kiss was? The beginning of a seduction?"

She shrugged, nothing casual about the gesture. "It is our wedding night. I thought—"

"We're friends. I wouldn't rush you like that."

He was only a few feet behind her now. She sensed his puzzled gaze drilling into her back, trying to discern what had panicked her. This would be a perfect time to tell him as her sister had encouraged her. Then she remembered some of the whispers said behind her back—*Maybe she had asked for it. Maybe she'd led him on. They had been dating.* She knew in her heart she hadn't asked to be raped, but the shame of the act clung to her as though it were a second skin. Could she have done something differently to prevent it? Why couldn't she have seen it coming? She had dated the man for several weeks, known him much longer, or so she'd thought.

"Tory, we talked about our marriage one day—being real in every sense. Have you changed your mind?"

Yes. No! How could she answer him when she was so torn up inside? She didn't know what she wanted. What a mess!

"Have you, Tory?"

She wheeled around and faced him, praying her expression was neutral, that none of the anguish twisting her stomach was visible. She never wanted to hurt this special man, but she was afraid she would. "No—one day." She looked toward Mirabelle's stall, then back into his eyes. "Please be patient. We haven't known each other long. Give me time."

One corner of his mouth lifted in a grin. "I had intended to do that very thing. A kiss isn't making love, Tory."

She sucked in a deep breath and held it for a few seconds before releasing it. "I know. It's just that I haven't dated much. I've been so busy and..." She let her words trail off into the silence, hoping he drew the conclusion she'd led a sheltered life, which was true for the past four years, and even before that.

"I understand."

You do? She almost said the words out loud but

stopped herself before she revealed her doubts. Instead she said, "I think these past few weeks are finally catching up with me. I'm overreacting. I'm sorry, Slade."

"You have nothing to be sorry for. It will take a while for us to adjust to living under the same roof. And I agree. It has been a long few weeks. I think I'm gonna turn in now."

"I'll be up to the house soon."

She watched him stride toward the entrance, his bearing suggesting the same weariness she felt. No matter how much she wanted to deny it, there had been a hurt expression in his eyes she'd glimpsed for a brief moment before he had managed to mask it. He didn't really understand. How could he when there were times she didn't?

She spun about to stare out the back door, looking toward the heavens. *Dear God, I hurt Slade tonight. Please help me to make this marriage work. I'm in over my head. I don't want to fail.*

Bright light pricked her eyelids. Tory slowly opened her eyes to find not only sunlight flooding her bedroom but Mindy sitting on her bed with a huge grin on her face.

"What time is it?" Tory raised herself up on her elbows, the fog of sleep clouding her mind.

"Se-ven."

"Seven!" Tory bolted straight up and peered at the clock on her beside table. "I overslept."

Mindy surveyed the room. "Where's—Dad-dy?"

"Uh—"

‘‘Right here, hon.’’ Slade lounged against the doorjamb, cradling a mug in his hand.

The scent of coffee teased Tory, steam wafting to the ceiling. She could use a big cup— Oh, my gosh! One hand went to smooth her hair while the other pulled the sheet up nearly to her chin. Her face felt as hot as the steaming cup of coffee.

Mindy eased herself down off the bed and trudged toward her father. ‘‘Go-ing—to see—Belle.’’

‘‘Hold it, young lady,’’ Slade said as his daughter squeezed past him. ‘‘We’re going to breakfast in town in—’’ he checked his watch ‘‘—forty-five minutes. You need to be back here and cleaned up.’’

‘‘I—wi-ll.’’ Mindy disappeared from sight.

Tory clutched the sheet to her chest, wishing she had on her flannel nightgown she wore in the winter. Instead, she was dressed in a flimsy pair of short pajamas whose top had thin straps. She would have to remember in the future that she now shared a house with a man.

‘‘Why didn’t you get me up earlier?’’ she asked, the hard edge to her voice she attributed to her nerves. It wasn’t every day she had a handsome man standing in her bedroom doorway, looking very appealing in a pair of tan slacks and navy blue Polo shirt that brought out the blue of his eyes. His conservatively cut hair was still damp from a shower, taken she realized in her bathroom. The thought again emphasized the awkward situation she found herself in.

‘‘Because you didn’t come back to the house until

after one. I thought you could use the sleep. You've been working nonstop for the past few weeks.''

Tory scanned the room for her robe. Where was it? When she spied it, it lay on a chair by the window. Too far for her to leap to and slip on without him noticing a few bare spots of skin. She had lived alone too long. She gestured toward the sky-blue cotton robe. ''Would you get that for me, please?'' The last word came out on a husky whisper, barely audible across the room.

One brow rose, his eyes locked with hers. Then he shrugged away from the door, strode to the chair and snatched up the short robe. When he brought her the garment, a smile was deep in his expression.

She grabbed the robe and slipped it on. When she stood on trembling legs to belt it, she noticed that the blue material didn't cover nearly enough of her legs. But it would have to do until she could get rid of her...*husband.* The word swirled in her mind.

When she faced Slade, she felt better prepared to carry on a conversation. He moved back to the doorway, his left shoulder cushioned again against the wooden frame. Slowly he lifted the mug to his lips and sipped, his gaze never leaving hers.

She swallowed several times, sure that if she spoke, her voice would come out a squeak. ''I hope you made a large pot of that,'' she finally said, and was pleased to note the strength in her words.

''Yes. I can get you some.''

''No, I'll get dressed and be in the kitchen in a few minutes.''

When he left, he pulled the door closed and Tory

hurried to throw on her new black jeans and a white blouse. After stuffing her feet into her tennis shoes, she headed for the bathroom to brush her teeth and wash her face. She entered the kitchen ten minutes later.

Slade had a cup of coffee poured for her and sitting on the table next to him. He tossed aside the newspaper and watched her cross the kitchen and sit in the chair opposite him. She slid the mug toward her, cupping her hands around it and bringing it to her lips. The strong brew slipped down her throat, giving her system a jolt of needed caffeine.

When she felt fortified with coffee, she rested her elbows on the table and said, "We need to discuss what we're going to say to Mindy about our situation. I gather by her question this morning you haven't said anything to her about why we got married."

"I told her we wanted to create a home for her, which is the truth."

"Yes, but she thinks we share a bedroom." Tory took another sip of her coffee. "She wasn't here when you moved in your things."

"I suppose you're right." His brow furrowed. "I hadn't thought to say anything to her. I don't want her to worry about us being a family."

"Still we need to say something to her about why we aren't sleeping in the same bedroom."

"I could always say I snore."

"Do you?"

He lifted his shoulders in a shrug. "I don't know. Carol never said anything about it."

"After our breakfast with my family, maybe we'll be able to talk with Mindy, together."

"Okay, together."

The smile he sent her doubled her heartbeat. He made the word *together* sound like a promise of things to come. She downed the rest of the coffee. "I'd better check on the horses before we leave."

"I was down there a while ago. Gus has everything under control. He came early so you wouldn't have to do anything today."

"But—"

"Tory, he wanted to do something special for you since you got married yesterday, so he's putting in some extra time."

She couldn't remember when she hadn't needed to go to the barn and take care of the horses. She wasn't sure she knew what to do with the leisure time.

"Relax. We'll be leaving for town in a few minutes anyway. Why don't you read the paper?" Slade slid a section toward her.

"When did I start getting the newspaper? I never have time to read it."

"I started its delivery today."

"Oh" was all she could manage to say. She wondered what else in her life would change because of this man.

"Gus—spect-ing—me." Mindy stuffed the rest of her turkey sandwich into her mouth, her cheeks ballooning.

"You aren't going anywhere, young lady, until

we're finished with lunch.'' Slade downed the last of his iced tea.

Putting her hand to her mouth, Mindy mumbled something and pointed to the sack with Tory's lunch inside.

''Tory can wait a few minutes while you chew your food properly.''

His daughter picked up her glass of milk and took several gulps. ''I—told—Tor-ee—I'd—bring—uh—lunch.''

''And you will, after you and I have a little talk.''

''But—Dad-dy—'' A pout formed on her mouth.

''What?''

''Can't—we—la-ter?''

''When? I can't seem to get you to sit long enough even to eat.''

Mindy pushed away her empty plate and leaned one elbow on the table, resting her chin in her palm. Her pout grew.

He really was tickled his daughter had a renewed interest in life, but she hardly stopped long enough to say hi to him. He'd been trying for the past few days to have a heart-to-heart with her about his marriage to Tory ever since he and Tory had discussed it on Saturday. He'd come home today from work just so he could before the afternoon riding lessons began. And now he felt as though he needed to hog-tie his daughter to get her to listen. Maybe he and Tory could make sure they rose before Mindy and went to bed after her. Usually that wouldn't be a problem, but every once in a while his daughter got up in the middle of the night.

"I wanted to explain why Tory and I aren't slee—" *Hold it! That isn't the way I want to tell Mindy.* Heat suffused his face as he thought of all the potential questions he could get from Mindy if he had continued. He wasn't ready for a discussion with his daughter of how babies were made. Truth be told, he never would be. *Isn't that what mommies do?* Sweat beaded his brow. "I mean why we aren't sharing a bedroom."

"That's—kay."

He sagged against the back of the chair. "It is?"

"Tor-ee—plain."

"She did?" Couldn't he come up with more than two-word questions?

Mindy grinned. "She—hogs—the bed."

He almost said, "She does?" but thankfully stopped himself before the first word came out. Sweat rolled down his face. He brushed away the salty trail. This father-daughter talk wasn't going the way he'd planned. But then he'd really not had this planned out. He'd come into this discussion with one thing on his mind: to get it over with as quickly as possible. He didn't want his daughter to know the real reasons Tory and he had married. It would worry and upset Mindy, which were two things he was determined not to do.

"When did Tory tell you?" he asked, deciding he and Tory needed to work on their communications better.

"To-day." Mindy struggled to her feet. "Can—I—go?"

"Sure." He watched his daughter slowly make her

way to the back door, her left foot still dragging behind her. The sight, as always, wrenched his heart. If only he had been able to avoid the accident. If nothing else, he should be the one recovering, not Mindy.

After taking the dishes to the sink and rinsing them off, he headed for the barn to start that communicating he and Tory needed to do. He found her finishing up with the blacksmith. Tory, even in hot weather, wore long jeans and riding boots with a short-sleeve plaid shirt and a beautifully designed leather belt her father had given her at Christmas. Her hair was pulled back in its usual ponytail with auburn wisps framing her face, void of any makeup but with a healthy glow to her cheeks and a smattering of freckles across the bridge of her nose. The way she looked amplified the woman he was getting to know—honest, caring, down-to-earth.

He waited to approach her until after the man left. When she saw him, her face lit with a smile that warmed him. He liked that she was glad to see him.

"Did you and Mindy have a nice lunch?"

"Yes, and it was informative."

"How so?"

"My daughter informs me that you hog the bed."

"Oh, that." The color in her cheeks deepened to a nice scarlet shade. "I know we talked about discussing it together, but we could never seem to find the right time. So when Mindy and I got to talking and I realized you hadn't said anything, I did. Was that why you came home in the middle of the day?"

"Yep." He stepped a little closer and lowered his

voice so Gus and Mindy who were down at the other end of the barn didn't hear, "Well, do you?"

"What?"

"Hog the bed?"

Her brown eyes grew round before she veiled them and turned away to pick up a wooden box at her feet. "I guess so."

"You don't know."

She cradled the box to her chest and stabbed him with an exasperated look. "It's not like I watch myself sleep. I do sometimes find myself waking up at odd angles across the middle of the bed. Why?"

"Just curious. I want to know the little and big things about my wife."

Wife. The word seemed to jolt Tory if the widening of her eyes meant anything. She still wasn't used to it or the fact that she was married to him. If truth be known, neither was he.

She started walking toward the tack room. He followed. At the door she twisted around and eyed him.

"I thought with the expansion, you'd need to get back to work."

He leaned one shoulder against the wall by the tack room and crossed his ankles. "Tired of me already?" He glanced at his watch. "We've only been married three days, one hour and fifteen minutes."

"You want to spend time with me?"

Beneath the question Slade noted the hint of vulnerability that crept into Tory's voice. He wanted her to trust him enough to tell him what had happened in her past that made her unsure, especially of men.

Several things came to mind, but until she confided in him, it was only speculation on his part.

"You're my wife. Isn't that what husbands and wives do?"

"You tell me. I've never been married." The corners of her mouth began to twitch as she took up his playful mood.

He folded his arms across his chest as though he would be hanging around for a long time. "Well, I don't have a vast knowledge, but I think so."

"You can always help me muck out a stall."

"I'm thinking more along the lines of a date."

"Don't you have it all backward? You're supposed to date a woman, *then* marry her." Laughter tinged her voice.

He liked seeing her smile and laugh. "What can I say? I'm an unconventional kind of guy."

"So you want me to go out on a date with you."

He nodded. "Without Mindy. Just you and me." The second he made the suggestion, a wariness entered her expression, which she quickly covered. But he'd seen it. "Don't get me wrong. I love my daughter and like spending time with her, but I want our marriage to work. That means we need to get to know each other well, keep the communication lines open."

"Who'd stay with Mindy?"

"Gus."

"Gus?" She said the name loud enough that the older man at the back of the barn with Mindy perked up and called out to Tory.

"Do you need something?" Gus stepped toward them.

"Uh—" She shot Slade a "help me" look.

Slade pivoted toward the older man. "We were just discussing your offer to baby-sit Mindy one evening so Tory and I could go out."

"When?" Mindy came out of Belle's stall.

"We're not sure yet, sweetheart. Would you be okay with that?"

"Yes!" His daughter pumped her arm in the air.

Slade turned back to Tory who stood slightly to the side and behind him. "So?"

"When did you and Gus make this arrangement? He's gone when you arrive home."

Home. The word had come so naturally from her that its implication made Slade pause for a few seconds. The farm was becoming his home and it was definitely Mindy's. "At the wedding. It was another one of his gifts to us. Perfect if you ask me. Mindy adores him, thinks of him as a grandfather."

"But—" Her protest died on her lips.

Slade wanted to take her into his arms and smooth away the tiny frown lines on her forehead. Remembering the kiss they had shared only reinforced his desire to embrace her. But he didn't. He resumed lounging against the wall, waiting for her to say something.

"I guess we could go out to dinner sometime this week. I'll have to ask Gus when he's available."

"Wednesday, Thursday and Friday nights."

"You know already?"

"Yep. He told me those were the nights he's usually free. Monday night is his book club and Tuesday he goes bowling.''

''My gosh, you know more about Gus than I do, and I work with him every day.''

''See. That's what I want to avoid with us. I want to know what your favorite color is. What movies you like to see. Do you read?''

''Yellow. What is your favorite color?''

''Green.''

''I like comedies and I love to read when I can find the time.''

He pushed away from the wall. ''This is good. It's a start. But there is so much more, and since we're sharing living space, I figure we should get to know each other.''

''Okay. How about Thursday night? My riding lessons are over with by five that evening.''

''Then it's a date. I'll tell Gus to stay late on Thursday. Where would you like to go?''

''To tell you the truth I haven't been to too many places in Cimarron City. I'll let you pick.''

''Surprise you?''

''So long as I know what to wear. I'll let Gus know for you.''

''Great. I need to get back to work before my secretary files a missing-person report.'' As he strode away, he whistled some tune he'd heard earlier on the radio, a lightness in his heart.

Humming a song she'd heard at church last Sunday, Tory appraised her outfit in the full-length mirror on her closet door. The soft pastel-blue rayon dress emphasized her narrow waist with a wide belt of the same material adorned in sequins and beadwork in flower designs. Along the scooped neckline and hem were the same flower decorations. She drew the white shawl about her shoulders and turned one final time to make sure she looked all right, the full skirt billowing out, then falling to below her knees when she stopped and faced the mirror again. Fortifying herself with a deep gulp of oxygen, she checked her hair, styled in a French braid that hung down her back. A few wisps framed her face, devoid of most makeup except pink lipstick and dark mascara.

A knock sounded at her door. She jumped. "Yes?"

"Are you ready?" Slade asked without opening the door.

"Yes, I'll be out in a sec." Tory glanced back at herself. Was she ready to go out on her first date in over four years? Even though Slade was her husband, she felt as though this was their first date. Her nerves were jittery, her mouth dry—just as if she'd never shared a house with the man.

When she entered the living room, Gus whistled and Mindy clapped, bouncing up and down on the couch.

Tory scanned the room. "Where's Slade?"

"Right here."

She whirled toward the sound of his deep voice. He stood in the doorway into the kitchen, his gaze traveling slowly up the length of her.

He let out his own whistle. ‘‘You look great. Ready?’’

The male appreciation she saw in his eyes robbed her of the ability to speak. She swallowed several times and finally managed, ‘‘Yes.’’

‘‘I left the information of where we’re going, by the phone, Gus.’’

‘‘You two go out and have fun. Miss Mindy and I are going to have our own fun. I’ve got some movies we’re gonna watch, and some popcorn.’’

‘‘Bedtime is nine, Mindy. Don’t give Gus any trouble about going to bed.’’

Mindy beamed, her hands folded in her lap. ‘‘I won’t.’’

Slade gave Mindy a kiss, then Tory did.

As she and Slade walked toward the front door, she heard Mindy ask Gus, ‘‘Can—I have—a soda?’’

Slade paused, said, ‘‘Just a minute,’’ and went back to the living room. ‘‘No caffeine, Mindy, or you’ll never get to sleep.’’

‘‘But—Dad-dy—’’

Slade held up his hand. ‘‘Fruit juice, young lady.’’

‘‘Oo-kay.’’

Tory could imagine the pout on Mindy’s mouth as she agreed. If they let the little girl, Mindy would drink sodas all day long. She definitely had a sweet tooth. The thought of Mindy settled her nerves. When Slade returned to her side, Tory sent him a smile, grateful for his laid-back ways and his innate understanding.

When she slid into the passenger’s side of Slade’s car, she followed his progress around to the driver’s side, admiring his self-confidence conveyed in how he carried himself, the pride he took in his appearance. He looked dynamite tonight, dressed in a charcoal-gray suit with a white shirt and a red tie.

"I'm guessing from the way we're dressed that we're going to a nice restaurant tonight," Tory said as Slade pulled out onto the main highway into town.

"It's the new one out on Old Baker's Road."

"The restaurant they made out of the Whitney's Flour Mill?"

He nodded. "I hear the food is delicious. I thought we could check it out before your parents and sister's family come back to town during the Fourth of July weekend."

"You don't have to take them out to dinner. They don't expect that."

"I want to get to know them, too. Gus has already agreed to baby-sit one of those evenings so just the adults can go out."

"I know my sister will be thrilled."

"It's good for a couple to go out by themselves every once in a while. I want us to at least once a month."

A couple! Once a month! Oh, my. She knew that what Slade thought was right. Each day she was married to him made it seem more real than the day before. Sometimes she found herself wanting to pinch herself to see if she would wake up from a dream. Just a month ago she wouldn't have thought of herself as someone's wife or mother and certainly not half of a couple.

At the new restaurant the sound of the stream behind the old mill lent a tranquil quality to the evening. The sun dipped behind the tall maples and oaks along the west side, creating shadows as night grew closer. The fresh scent of earth and forest saturated the warm air and the coolness of the surrounding towering trees chased away some of the heat of a June day.

The atmosphere was romantic and further enhanced by the quaintness of the restaurant, its decor rustic.

It was as though they had stepped back into the 1800s. Inside, Tory took in the candlelit tables with white tablecloths covered with crystal, china and silver. Each place setting gleamed with the flames from the candles.

Slade assisted Tory into her chair at a table for two in a corner alcove. The picture window afforded her a view of the small stream rippling over rocks. Perfect. She could tell Slade had taken care in selecting the place to eat for their first date. The idea pleased her.

After placing their orders, Tory relaxed in her chair. ''I have to admit I don't eat filets too often. Too expensive on my budget.''

''That's all changed now, Tory. We're married. What is mine is yours.''

Half of a couple, she reminded herself, still not used to that concept. After the incident four years ago she hadn't thought that would ever happen. Of course, her marriage wasn't the normal kind.

Next to her he leaned forward. ''What kind of expansion plans do you have for the Bright Star Stables?''

''Expansion? None. All I've ever wanted to do was pay my bills. I've never thought beyond that.''

''What if you could dream? What would you like to do with the stables?''

Tory blew out a breath of air, all the possibilities she'd pushed to the back of her mind flooding her now. ''I'd like to have an indoor riding ring so I could have lessons all year long.''

''Done.''

''Done? What do you mean?''

''I want you to start making plans to build one. I think that's an excellent way for me to invest my money.''

''But—'' Stunned, Tory couldn't think of anything else to say.

''Don't forget, Mindy will benefit more than anyone if you have an indoor riding ring.''

Her shock still firmly gripped her. ''You have that kind of money?'' Again she realized she really didn't know that much about Slade—except that he was a kind, loving father and a good friend.

''I haven't had a chance to tell you yet, but my company was just awarded a big contract I've been pushing for this past year. An international food company has contracted us to make all their plastic containers.''

''Then this is a celebration tonight.''

He raised his water glass. ''To both of our dreams.''

What were his dreams? she wondered, taking a sip

of her ice water, her gaze bound to Slade's. Thankfully the liquid was cold to chase away the heat that permeated her.

"I do mean it, Tory, about making plans for the indoor ring. I'd like it built by next winter. That way, Mindy can continue with her riding therapy."

"I'm not even sure where to begin."

"How about with contacting some contractors about bidding on the indoor ring? The company that did my expansion work was excellent and reasonable." He covered her hand on the table. "It's about time your dreams come true."

The feel of his hand over hers riveted her senses to the roughness of his fingertips and the warmth of his flesh. "What are your dreams?" she murmured, her shock slowly wearing off to be replaced with a reality, a reality that centered around Slade and his daughter. They were an intricate part of her life now. Her family. If only she could take the next step. Time was running out on her dream to have a child of her own, if she was ever able to.

"I want Mindy to be whole again."

Before he withdrew his hand, Tory felt the tension in his touch. "Is that all?"

"That's the only one I can afford right now."

Puzzled, she tilted her head to the side. "Why?"

"My life is on hold until Mindy is well."

"She is well. She's no longer having seizures."

He gritted his teeth, the line of his jaw hard. "She struggles every day. I don't call that well."

"She doesn't see it as struggling."

His eyes became pinpoints, his lips pressing together. He remained silent, the atmosphere at the table suddenly frosty. Tory fought the strong urge to touch his arm, instinctively knowing he would pull away. He didn't see his daughter in the same light as she did.

Tory unfolded her napkin and placed it in her lap, needing to do something with her hands. "Mindy wanted me to ask you to come to church with us this Sunday. Will you?" She hoped the topic change would ease the strain that sprang up between them.

He cloaked his expression, releasing a deep sigh. "I don't know. I may have to work on Sunday."

"Work?"

"Yes, with that new contract I'll have some things I'll need to iron out."

"You have an open invitation to come with us any Sunday you can. Mindy has made some friends she wants you to meet."

The tense set to his shoulders relaxed. He lifted his gaze to hers. "To be truthful, I don't know if church is for me."

"Because of the accident?"

He nodded, taking a deep swallow of his water.

"God hasn't let you down. He just may have a different plan for you."

"Don't you understand? It's never been about me. It's about Mindy and—" He clamped his mouth shut and looked away.

About his deceased wife. He'd walked away from the accident. She hadn't. Mindy hadn't. Tory reached out and laid her hand on his arm, praying he wouldn't pull away. He stiffened for a few seconds.

When the tension melted from his expression, his posture, Tory felt a connection to him that went straight to her heart and bound them together for several beats.

Maybe she had been brought into his life not only to help Mindy but to help him. Slade's hurt went deeper than she suspected he realized. *Lord, show me the way to help Slade heal, to forgive himself for surviving.*

Shaking his head, he stared at her hand on his arm. "This was supposed to be a celebration, a beginning for us. How did everything get so turned around?"

Tory smiled. "I think we were talking about our dreams."

Placing his hand over hers, he linked gazes. "I want to help make yours come true."

And I want to help make yours come true. But Tory wouldn't voice her wish out loud.

"So I want you to start right away on the indoor riding ring."

Tory thought about her other wish and wondered if Slade could help her with that one. Her fear had been with her for so long she was afraid it wasn't possible.

Chapter Eight

"Do you—think—Dad-dy—will—let me go to—" Mindy scrunched up her face and thought for a few seconds "—sch-ool?"

Tory shifted the bag of clothes from one hand to the other in order to open the truck door for Mindy. The child pushed her walker away and lifted herself into the front seat. "Do you want to go back when school starts?"

Mindy screwed her face up into another thoughtful expression. After a minute, she nodded. "I—miss my—" she searched for the right word "—friends."

Tory closed the door and folded up the walker to put in the bed of the truck. Remembering the battle she'd had that morning to get Mindy to use the walker brought a smile to her mouth. By the end of their trek through the mall the little girl had been leaning heavily on the walker. Even though she doubted Mindy would say she was glad she'd insisted they take the walker, Tory was sure Mindy was thankful. She hated admitting she still needed occasional help, especially if she was going to be doing a lot. She still tired easily and didn't want to take a nap when she needed to. Gus had changed that. He'd declared one day how important his catnaps were to him each afternoon. Since then Mindy had taken her "catnaps" without complaint. Slade and his daughter were a lot alike, Tory was discovering. Slade didn't think he needed any help, either. But he was hurting, and she intended to help him any way she could.

After stowing the walker, Tory slipped behind the steering wheel and started the truck. "Then we'll just have to convince your father how important going to school is to you."

"Let's—go see—him—now," Mindy said, in all the eagerness she was known for.

Tory checked the clock on the dashboard. "It's close to lunchtime. We could take him out to eat."

"Yeah! Sur-sur—" Mindy struggled for the word and ended up frowning.

"Does your dad like surprises?"

"Yes! Sur-prise—him."

"Then that's our next stop before we go to speech therapy."

Mindy smiled, displaying the new gaping hole where her loose tooth had been the evening before. She dug into her purse and produced her five-dollar bill from the tooth fairy. "I'll—buy."

Tory headed toward the company headquarters about a mile from the mall. "I've got a better idea. Let's get your dad to treat us."

"Oo-kay. I—can—get—can-dy—la-ter."

"I was thinking more along the lines of ice cream before we head back to the ranch."

"Yes!" Mindy clapped.

When they arrived at Donaldson Corporation, Mindy hurried ahead, her fatigue forgotten in her haste to see her father. Tory quickly followed, never having been to Slade's headquarters. She glanced up at the four-story building and had visions of running around lost in the large place. One of the security guards waved at Mindy as she made her way toward the hallway off to the left.

"I'm with Mindy," Tory said to the guard.

"You must be Mrs. Donaldson."

Hearing her new name sent a rush of excitement through her. She really hadn't thought much about her being Tory Donaldson. It had only been two weeks since their marriage. "Yes, I am."

Mindy disappeared through a door at the end of the corridor. Tory quickened her pace, eager to see Slade in his work environment. The company was so much a part of him as her riding stable was a part of her.

When Tory entered the outer office, the secretary behind the desk smiled at her. "Mindy's inside with her father, Mrs. Donaldson." The older woman stood and extended her hand. "I'm Mrs. Hardmeyer. I'm sorry I couldn't make your wedding."

After greeting Slade's secretary, Tory approached the double doors that led to his office. When she stepped inside, she found Mindy sitting on his lap, giggling. "We came to steal you away for lunch."

"Lunch? Already?" Slade glanced down at a gold

clock on his desk. "I've been so busy I'd forgotten the time."

"Then you'll let us take you out." Tory scanned the large office with a bank of windows behind Slade's massive oak desk, littered with stacks of files and papers. Off to the left sat a cozy area for conversations with a long brown leather couch and two comfortable-looking plaid chairs. Bookcases were along the other side of the room. The office reflected Slade's personality.

"Plee-ze, Dad-dy."

He grinned, his eyes gleaming. "How can I refuse an invitation from two lovely ladies?"

"You—can't." Gripping the desk, Mindy slid off her father's lap and stood next to him. "Rea-dy."

"I guess I am." Laughter laced his voice as he rose.

"One day when we have more time I'd like a tour of your company."

"Just let me know and I'll set aside some time."

"Me—too."

Slade ruffled his daughter's hair. "You, too, sweetheart. We'll make it a family outing."

"Like—uh—lun-ch."

Walking toward the exit with Slade and Mindy reinforced the feeling of family that was growing in Tory. She settled into Slade's car, parked near the entrance, and let him pick the restaurant while Mindy told her father about their shopping trip. With Gus at the stables, she could afford to take some time off and enjoy this outing with Mindy and Slade. She didn't have to worry like she used to about what she had to do at the ranch.

"I—got—new—dress—for—chur-ch."

"I bet you look pretty in it."

"Will—you—come? In play—Sun-day."

Slade shot Tory a narrowed look. She raised her eyebrows and shrugged.

"I'll see, sweetheart."

"Plee-ze," Mindy said from the back seat.

With tiny lines creasing his forehead, Slade maneuvered his car into a parking space next to a hamburger joint. "I'll be there to see you. What part are you playing?"

"Hor-se."

"Horse! What's the play about?"

"Noah's Ark. Mindy's representing the two horses. She wanted to since she rides them. Different pairs of animals are being played by one child since we don't have enough children to do two of every animal."

"Are you wearing a costume?" Slade asked, opening the door for Mindy to slide out of the back seat.

The little girl nodded. "Mrs. Pl-ank's—do-ing—it."

"Because I don't know how to sew other than sewing on a button in an emergency." Tory fell into step next to Mindy with Slade on his daughter's other side.

"That's okay. If you ask me to do anything other than change a light bulb around the house, I'd have to hire someone to do it."

While Mindy went ahead of them and stood in line behind a young boy and his mother, Tory hung back with Slade. "Are you okay about church on Sunday? The play isn't that big a deal. Some of the Sunday school classes have been working on it the past few weeks. They're going to perform in the rec hall on the stage after the nine o'clock service."

"I'm fine. It's a big deal to Mindy. I'll be there. Are you sure she'll be okay in front of an audience?"

"Yes. Will you come to the church service, too?"

He blew out a breath of air. "You're a very determined woman."

"Yes."

"We'll make it a family outing, then."

"Good." The pleasant warmth that coursed through her veins at Slade's mention of the word *family* caused a sharpening of her awareness of the man beside her. He might not be handy around the house, but she was beginning to depend on him, and that frightened her. Her emotions had been locked up so tight for a long time. She was afraid to release them and feel again, afraid her judgment somehow would be wrong again. Or that Slade wouldn't be able to accept her for whom she really was.

Tory started for Mindy. Slade placed a hand on her arm to halt her movements.

"Thanks for making this easy, Tory. I do feel we're becoming a family and Mindy thinks so. She told me last night while I was putting her to bed."

A tightness jammed her throat. She felt it, too. She might never have the children she wanted, but Mindy was like a daughter to her and this man was responsible. She owed him a lot, but she didn't know if she could ever totally be free of her past to unconditionally give of herself in a marriage. Slade deserved that.

"Thank you again for agreeing to go to church Sunday with us." Tory tore the fresh spinach and placed it in the large wooden salad bowl. "Mindy talked all day about you coming to see her be a horse in the play."

"Does she have a speaking part?" Slade opened the cabinet door and extracted the dinner plates.

"Yes." Pausing in chopping up a tomato, Tory glanced at her husband setting the table as though they had been working side by side in the kitchen for years instead of weeks. "Just a small part."

"But still, she's speaking in front of an audience." He shook his head. "I don't know if that's wise. What if someone laughs at how slow she speaks? What if she forgets her lines?"

Tory put her balled hands on her waist. "They won't, Slade Donaldson. And even if they did, we're here to help her get through it. You can't constantly protect Mindy from life."

Looking up, he frowned. "Frankly, I don't know that I've done such a great job of protecting my daughter from life so far."

"She wanted to do this play. I'm not sorry I told her yes."

"You should have checked with me."

"Then come to church with us each week and you'll know what's going on. If I'm going to be responsible for taking care of Mindy when you aren't here, then you'll have to trust my judgment about what is good for her.'' Her fingernails dug into her palms, remembering her own qualms earlier about her judgment.

''I do trust you.''

''Then quit acting like you don't. Mindy has enjoyed rehearsing with the others. No one has made fun of her. Not everyone is like those children in the mall.''

The tense set to his shoulders relaxed. The hard lines of his face smoothed. ''Did we just have our first fight?''

Tory dropped her hands to her sides. ''I guess we did.''

''Just like an old married couple.''

''Speak for yourself. I'm not old,'' she said with a laugh, needing to lighten the mood before she began to dream of them as a real old married couple.

''Seriously, I don't know if I'll ever stop worrying about Mindy and how people will receive her.''

''I know. That's part of being a parent. I worry, too.''

Slade finished setting the eating utensils on each bamboo place mat. Tory continued cutting the rest of the tomatoes, listening to him moving around the table. There were still times that it seemed strange to wake up in the morning and find Slade in the kitchen fixing the coffee or coming out of the only bathroom in the house after having taken a shower, his hair wet, dressed in a robe. When she had been in college, she'd shared an apartment her last two years. It was like that but of course different since Slade was a male.

"I'll get the barbecued chicken. It should be done by now."

Slade stood right behind her and the sudden sound of his voice so near her ear caused her to jump and gasp. Laying a hand against her chest, she drew in deep breaths and twisted about to look at him. "You scared me. I didn't hear you approach." The rapid beat of her heart still pounded against her rib cage. His lime scented aftershave swamped her senses.

"Sorry." He offered her a smile. "I didn't know making a salad could be so absorbing."

"Just thinking," she said, turning back to complete the task. The hand that held the knife trembled.

"Anything you'd like to share with me?"

No way. "You know Dave Patterson is meeting with me on Monday about the plans for the indoor riding ring."

"He's a good man. I think you'll be impressed with his work."

"Mindy can't wait. She told me once we have the indoor ring she can ride every day even when it's raining or snowing."

Slade picked up the large platter and walked to the back door. "That's the whole idea."

"I'll go find Mindy and have her wash up."

As Slade disappeared outside, Tory put the salad bowl in the middle of the table then headed toward the front porch where she'd left Mindy earlier to play. The heat of a summer day blasted her when she stepped out onto the porch. A breeze ruffled the stray strands of her ponytail but did nothing to relieve the warmth.

She scanned the area. "Mindy." Walking to the edge of the porch, she searched the yard. Mindy knelt by a bush along the front of the house, her face pressed down as she looked beneath the shrubbery. "Mindy, what are you doing?"

"A ba-by." Mindy scooted closer to whatever she was looking at.

One of the kittens? Tory hurried down the steps to where Mindy was. Standing a few feet behind her and to the left, she stooped down to see what the child was so fascinated by. Curled in a ball was a small black fluffy animal with white markings.

Mindy started to reach for the animal. Tory shouted, "No."

The fluffy ball uncurled, his dark eyes opening. It hissed, arching its back, its raised tail pointed toward Mindy. Before Tory could grab the child and yank her away, the baby skunk sprayed the arm still reaching toward it. Mindy jumped back, landing on her bottom. The skunk scurried away, disappearing under the house, its horrible odor left behind.

"Ph-ew!" Mindy waved her arm around, the pungent smell quickly spreading.

Tory covered her mouth and nose, her eyes blinking from the intense odor emanating from Mindy.

"I—thought—it was—a new—kit-ten." Tears welled in the little girl's eyes. "I—uh—stink."

"I guess we found out what's living under the house. A family of skunks." With tears streaming down Mindy's face, Tory couldn't resist hugging the child, keeping her sprayed arm away from her. ‘‘We’ll take care of this.’’

‘‘The—play!’’

‘‘By Sunday. I promise.’’

‘‘Mindy, Tory, what’s going on?’’ Slade sniffed the air. ‘‘I smell a skunk.’’

‘‘Those raccoons under the house are really skunks.’’

‘‘We have a problem.’’

‘‘That’s an understatement.’’ Tory gestured toward Mindy. ‘‘She got just a little too close.’’

He made his way toward them, a grimace forming on his face. ‘‘What should we do about the smell?’’

Tory started walking with Mindy toward the house. ‘‘I’ll need you to go into town and buy several bottles of hydrogen peroxide. I have one bottle but I don’t know if it will do the trick.’’

‘‘Hydrogen peroxide?’’

Tory waved her hand. ‘‘Go. I’ll explain later.’’

Inside she had Mindy remove her shirt. ‘‘I’ll put this outside until I can get rid of it.’’

After that Mindy sat on the lip of the tub while Tory went about mixing up a homemade remedy. Using the hydrogen peroxide she had on hand, she combined it with baking soda and liquid dishwashing soap. While foaming, she spread it on Mindy’s sprayed arm and hoped for the best.

Thirty minutes later, Slade hurried into the house with five bottles of hydrogen peroxide, ready to do battle with the odor. He stopped when he saw Mindy, dressed and smiling. He sniffed the air. The skunk scent still lingered but definitely not as strong as before.

"What happened?"

"I had enough hydrogen peroxide to take care of it this time. Thankfully the skunk sprayed Mindy's arm. Not too large an area. We'll treat the area again. The odor should wear off completely by Sunday. The more important question is what are we going to do about the family living under the house?"

"Good question. Skunks are definitely out of my expertise."

"I'm not sure, either. We could try loud noises or bright lights. It may not be easy."

"Well, we need to do something. I don't want a repeat of today." Slade's nose wrinkled up, trying to get used to the faint odor that peppered the air as a reminder of their guests under the house.

"I—won't—bo-ther—again. Prom-ise."

"I know, honey. But I don't think it's wise to have a family of skunks living under the house. Do you think a loud noise will work?"

Tory shrugged.

Slade retrieved the stereo from the kitchen and placed it on the bench on the deck. He switched on a radio station with rock-and-roll music and turned it up loud.

"If that doesn't drive them away, it sure will take care of me," he shouted over the din.

Back inside the house the noise was marginally softer. At least they didn't have to yell at each other to hear. But the sound of the bass vibrated the house and dinner was eaten in quiet to the background music of the eighties and nineties.

Afterward Tory began clearing the dishes. ''Why don't I ask around and find out what might work? I don't think I can take much more of this noise.''

''Just our luck. We'll drive ourselves nuts while the skunks have a good old time.'' Slade went outside and switched off the radio.

Silence blissfully filled the air. Tory released a long sigh. Then she suddenly heard a crash and ran toward the back door. Slade flew over the railing and jogged toward the hose. He turned it on and pointed it toward a large skunk scurrying across the grass. From the safety of the other side of the yard Slade tried to drive the animal away. Instead, he ended up drenching the ground and forming several mud puddles.

The skunk disappeared into the meadow, out of reach of the water spray. Slade set his face in determination and stretched the hose as far as he could. It didn't do any good. The water fell short of its target.

Mindy and Tory stood on the deck, watching the battle. Tory covered her mouth, trying to contain her laughter. Because the nozzle wasn't on tight enough, it leaked water from the hose connection and ran down Slade's arm and onto his pants and tennis shoes.

''Dad-dy—fun-ny.''

''Yes, very.''

He dropped the hose and strode to the deck. ''This

is war. She has to come back and I'm gonna be ready for her."

"I'll get you a towel. Don't forget I can make some calls and see what we can do about the skunks."

"I think she was actually mocking me," Slade grumbled while heading back to the hose with a lawn chair in his hands.

Mindy giggled.

"I know, Mindy. No one will believe he is standing guard waiting for a skunk to return home."

Tory went into the house and grabbed a large towel. When she walked through the kitchen to the back door, she noted the stacked dishes by the sink. She shook her head and stepped outside to the sight of Slade bolting out of the lawn chair, switching on the hose, and running toward the returning skunk. His feet hit one of the mud puddles and flew up into the air. Slade landed on his back, staring at the sky, with the hose in his hand, squirting water upward like a fountain. It fell in sheets onto his prone body, thoroughly soaking him.

Mindy doubled over laughing while Slade pushed himself to his elbows, water dripping off him. The skunk disappeared under the house. The hose continued to drench the ground around Slade.

Tory hurried to the faucet and twisted it off. "Stay there. I'll get some more towels."

"Oh—Dad-dy—you're—too—much." Mindy started toward the stairs to the backyard.

"I agree, Mindy, but I think you'd better stay here. It looks pretty slippery out there." Tory waited until

Mindy stopped by the railing before she headed back inside for some more towels.

She knew there was a competitive edge to Slade, but with a skunk? He was too much, Tory thought, her own laughter bubbling to the surface as she recalled his soaked, muddy body. When she returned to the deck, Mindy held the hose and was spraying her father clean. He pirouetted slowly, allowing her to reach his back, as well. When he was rinsed off, he took a towel from Tory and turned the faucet off. The sounds of two animals fighting came from under the house.

He arched one brow, a frown marring his features. ''It's catching.''

''Like—a cold?'' Mindy asked with a giggle.

Slade shivered, hugging his arms to him. ''If I don't get inside and changed, I'll get a cold,'' he grumbled.

''It's ninety degrees out here. I don't think so.''

Slade sloshed up the steps. ''It could happen. I've heard of summer colds.''

''Hold it. Where do you think you're going? You're still dripping wet. And those shoes!''

He held up his hands. ''I'll take them off. Promise.'' He bent down and removed his tennis shoes and socks, then draped them over the chair to dry. Taking another towel, he ran it down his body one more time. ''Okay?'' He spread his arms wide and turned in a full circle.

''Fine.''

When Slade disappeared into the house, Mindy

looked over the railing at the crawl space where the skunks lived. ''They—don't—sound—hap-py.''

''If your father has anything to do about it, they won't be until they move on.''

''The—ba-by was—cute.''

''Melinda Donaldson, you better not try to hold one again.''

Mindy stuck her lower lip out. ''I—won't.''

''Good.'' Tory clasped the child's shoulder and started for the back door. ''Now, we have a dinner to clean up. Do you think you can help me while your daddy is changing?''

''Yes!''

Together they entered the kitchen and began rinsing the dishes to put in the dishwasher. Tory thought back to the past few hours and even though nothing had gone according to plans, she had enjoyed herself. Combating the skunk problem had made them seem even more like a family. She relished that feeling.

Slade sat down next to Tory in the audience and leaned close. ''Are you sure about this?''

''Yes, Mindy will be fine. I got her in her horse costume and she knows her line.''

''Still—''

''Slade, stop worrying. You saw the children with Mindy. They have accepted her and she feels part of the group.''

Sighing, he settled back and crossed his arms as though steeling himself for the next twenty minutes.

The lights in the recreational hall dimmed and the audience of parents and friends quieted. The curtain on the stage opened, revealing a boy playing Noah standing in front of what was supposed to be the newly built ark, even though it was a cardboard cut-out. Soon the children appeared who represented the various animals of the world. When Mindy came on stage, dressed in brown burlap, a long tail of twined rope fastened to the back, Slade tensed, clasping Tory's hand and holding it hostage.

Mindy trudged toward Noah and stopped. "We—want to—join—you."

Tory heard the swoosh of air leave Slade when Mindy finished her line. He squeezed her hand, but instead of releasing his grasp, he kept it clasped. His hand surrounding hers felt right. He didn't let it go until the end when everyone clapped as the children took their bows.

He rose and stretched. "I'm glad that is over."

"Why?" Tory came to her feet.

"It's not easy holding your breath until your daughter makes her appearance." His mouth quirked in a lopsided grin.

"Holding your breath?"

"Not exactly the whole time, but it was hard to breathe properly when all I could do was worry if she would remember what to say. I definitely hope she doesn't want to go on stage as an actress. I don't think I could take it."

"Knowing you, you'll support anything Mindy wants to do."

"Dad-dy," Mindy called out a few feet from them. She weaved among the adults until she was standing next to Slade. "I—did—it!"

"Yes, you did, sweetheart. You're braver than I would be. I don't think I could get up in front of a group of people and recite lines."

"I—didn't—for-get one—word." Mindy's chest swelled, her chin lifted.

"Nope."

"I'm—get-ting—bread." Mindy crunched her face into a frown. "I mean—cake." She headed off into the crowd toward the table at the back of the recreational hall that had a large sheet cake on it with fruit punch next to it.

"Mmm. Chocolate cake sounds good." Slade eyed the pieces being sliced.

"I'm sure there'll be enough for the adults, too."

"You know I have a weakness for chocolate." He watched Mindy take a plate and a cup and walk toward a group of children sitting at a table.

"Is that your only weakness?"

"I do like ice cream and French fries. Both probably aren't too good for you."

"Oh, my, with weaknesses like those, you're in big trouble." Tory splayed her hand over her chest in mock shock.

A serious expression descended on Slade's face. "I wish that was all."

"What deep, dark secrets could you possibly have?" Tory asked, thinking of her own that she kept close to her heart.

"We all have secrets we want to protect."

"Not from God."

Slade's frown evolved into a scowl, his lips clamped together. When Reverend Nelson joined them, Slade relaxed his expression into a neutral one, but Tory saw the slight stiffening to his shoulders that indicated his tension. When had she come to know Slade so well? They had been married only a few weeks, and yet she knew his moods even when he was trying to mask them.

"It's good to see you at church, Slade." Reverend Nelson shook his hand. "I hope this means you'll be coming more often with Tory and Mindy."

"Possibly, when work permits."

"We could use someone with your expertise on our budget committee."

"I don't know if I have that kind of time."

"I hope you'll think about it. Tory, I like your idea about using your horses for the summer carnival. The kids will enjoy riding."

When the reverend left, Slade asked, "What summer carnival?"

"The one we'll be hosting over the Fourth of July weekend."

"Hosting!"

Tory automatically took a step back. "I know I should have said something sooner, but it was just decided yesterday. Once I volunteered the horses, the committee liked the idea of moving the carnival to the ranch. There's more room and I won't have to transport the horses. It's good advertisement for the riding stable especially now that it's being fixed up."

"But the Fourth is a week away."

"I know. Mindy will be excited."

"You mean she doesn't know yet?" His frown returned.

Tory closed the space between them, placing her hand on his arm. ''I haven't had a chance to tell her, either.''

''Sometimes I think I'm the last to know what's going on,'' he grumbled. ''How many people come to this carnival?''

''Probably over a hundred. The church uses it as a fund-raiser.''

''Have you volunteered me for any jobs?''

''Of course not. I hope you'll help me with the rides, but you don't have to do anything if you don't want to. In fact, you can spend the day at work if you want to escape.''

Slade snorted. ''Not if I want to come home to two ladies who will be speaking to me.''

''I'd better tell you also that my family has definitely decided to visit over that weekend. They come every year and believe me, this one will be no different.''

''Checking me out?''

Tory nodded.

''I can live with that. Thank goodness I didn't make any plans for the holiday.''

''I'm not used to running my plans by someone. I haven't had to before.''

''We're a family, Tory. Don't forget that.''

She inhaled a calming breath and braced herself. ''I also think we should go to Carol's grave site today after church. I know the past month or so has been hectic with you looking for a housekeeper then us getting married so suddenly.''

Slade closed his eyes for a few seconds, and when

he opened them again, Tory saw the anguish in his gaze.

"Mindy needs to say goodbye to her mother."

"I know. We'll go."

"Do you want me to go, too?"

"Do you want to?"

"Yes, we're a family, Slade. And don't forget that."

"Then let's get Mindy and go now."

The ride to the cemetery was done in silence with a quick stop at a grocery store for some fresh flowers. Slade pulled up to the grave site and helped Mindy from the back seat. Tory followed the pair to the marble headstone with Carol Marie Donaldson's name. Mindy put the assorted flowers in the vase at the base of the headstone, then stood back.

"They—die—with-out—wa-ter."

Tory scanned the area and found an outdoor faucet nearby. "We can fill the vase with some water before we leave."

With a somber expression, Slade placed his hands on Mindy's shoulders and stood behind her. "Mommy's buried here."

"She's—with—God—now."

"Yes, sweetheart."

"Can—she—hear—me?"

"I believe she can. I'm sure she's watching over you. She loved you very much."

Mindy leaned her head back until she stared at the sky above her. "Mom-my, I—love—you." Tears roughened her voice. "Tell—God—hi—for me. Good-bye, Mom-my."

Tory fought to keep her own tears at bay. *Carol, I promise I'll look out for Mindy and love her as you would,* Tory vowed, brushing the back of her hand across her cheeks.

Chapter Nine

The sun dipped below the tree line as Tory approached Slade by the fence. With his forearms propped on the top of the railing, he stared at the horses eating grass in the field. For the past three days he distanced himself from her until he hardly said a word tonight at dinner. Even Mindy had noticed and said something to her while she was putting her to bed.

''Are we having our second fight?'' she asked, stopping only an arm's length away from him.

He threw her a glance, then resumed watching the horses. ''No. What makes you think that?''

She shrugged. ''Oh, I don't know. Maybe the fact today we have exchanged no more than a handful of words.''

''Got things on my mind.''

''About the church carnival in a couple of days? I'm sorry I didn't consult you first. I—''

''I'm not upset about the carnival, Tory.''

She shifted so she faced him. "Then what are you upset about?"

He didn't look at her, but tension vibrated the air between them. The silence stretched to a full minute, and Tory began to wonder if he'd even heard her question.

"It's really not a secret. Today is the second anniversary of the car wreck." He leaned into the fence, his gaze still trained forward on the animals in the field.

The tension sharpened, cutting through Tory's defenses that were always erected. "And?"

He stabbed her with his narrowed gaze. "And what?"

"Anniversaries are for marriages, things like that, not a car wreck. It's not productive to look back like that."

"So you never look back and wonder what your life would be like if something didn't happen?"

His question caused Tory to suck in a deep breath. "Not if I can help it. Is that what you're doing? Wondering what your life would be like if the wreck had never happened?" She hadn't wanted the wreck ever to happen, either, but she couldn't keep the hurt from lacing her words.

"I was thinking about how different Mindy's life would be if she hadn't been in the wreck, if I had paid more attention and been able to avoid the truck."

"No matter how much you beat yourself up over this, accidents happen."

He turned toward her, lines creasing his brow.

"You don't understand! I was arguing with Carol about her going back to work. I should have been paying better attention. The last words my wife and I exchanged were said in anger."

Until Slade came to terms with his wife's death and the wreck, there was no chance for their marriage to work. She saw it in the pain that shadowed his eyes. She heard it in the anguish reflected in each of his words. She wanted to take him into her embrace and hold him close to her heart. She wanted to erase the ache he felt and replace it with hope. "She knows how you really felt."

"I broke my own rule. I never fought with Carol in front of Mindy. That day I did. I was tired, having put in a long day of negotiations with the union." He pivoted away, staring again at the horses. "I don't think my daughter remembers much about that day. But if she ever remembers the argument I was having with Carol, she'll blame me."

The torment in his voice shredded her composure. Tears clogged her throat. She stepped toward him and laid her hand on his shoulder. The muscles beneath her palm bunched. "Mindy loves you. Nothing is going to change that, Slade."

"I was driving and I walked away. No one else did."

She placed her other hand on his other shoulder. "Let God into your heart. Let Him heal you."

"What if you're too broken?"

As though they had a will of their own, her arms wound about him and she laid her head on his back. Too broken? She'd thought that at one time, lying in the hospital bed after her date had assaulted her physically and emotionally.

"No one's too broken for God to fix."

He straightened away from the fence, cupping her clasped hands. The quick rise and fall of his chest underscored the emotions churning inside him. Turning within the circle of her arms, he lifted her chin so his glittering gaze could seek hers. "I can't ask Carol for her forgiveness."

"Then ask God."

"I've forgotten how."

The sound of his voice, heavy with emotions, filled her with sorrow. Tory splayed her hand over his chest, feeling the rapid beating beneath her palm. "It's simple. Ask from the heart."

He plunged his fingers into her hair, loose and about her shoulders the way he liked it, and cradled her face between his hands. "You're an amazing woman."

"Slade, you are not to blame for what happened. Carol wouldn't want you to waste your life agonizing over something you can't change."

"Ah, your motto. Forget the past."

"Learn from the past but move on. You can't change what's happened, but you might have some control over what is to happen."

One corner of his mouth lifted. "That's why I'm focusing all my energy into making sure Mindy recovers." His hands fell away from her face.

She missed the warmth of his palms against her cheeks. For a few moments she'd felt connected to Slade. Now she felt the distance as he stepped back against the fence. "Mindy is recovering." But was he? He might not have been physically hurt in the wreck but he was emotionally. Would he ever heal? The brightness and hope of their future as a married couple dimmed.

"I know. I just want it to have happened yesterday. Patience has never been my strong suit." He took her hand and started for the house. "I could learn some from you. I've seen you with your students, with Mindy, with your horses. You have a great deal of patience. Want to share some with me?"

"I'm gonna need all I have to get through this carnival. I forgot what a big deal it was. The next few days will be hectic and I still have to see to my horses."

"Not to mention your family coming tomorrow."

"You don't mind, do you?"

He stopped at the bottom of the steps up to the front porch. "The question is, will your family mind? It's gonna be crowded here."

"Don't worry about them. Judy has a camper. The kids are going to stay out there while the adults are staying in the house."

"There are only three bedrooms, Tory."

"Oh."

With all that had been happening, she hadn't stopped to think about the sleeping arrangements. Three couples. Three bedrooms. That should be simple and it would be if she was sharing a bedroom with her husband.

"How do you want to deal with the situation?"

His question brought her anxiety to the surface. Share a bedroom—a bed with Slade. Or, tell her family about her arranged marriage. ''I don't know,'' she finally said, searching the dark shadows of his face for some kind of answer. In his blue eyes she saw support and comfort and drew strength from that.

''Ju-dy! Tor-ee!''

''I think the children found us.'' Judy brought the glass of lemonade to her lips and took a long drink.

Three heads appeared around the corner of the barn followed by three bodies. Ashley, Jamie and Mindy surrounded Judy and Tory. She and her sister were sitting in the shade of the barn, but it was still hot, the sun still up in the western sky.

Ashley placed her hand on her waist. ''We've been looking all over for you two.''

Judy's daughter reminded Tory so much of her big sister even down to the straight long blond hair and hazel eyes. ''We thought we would let the men prepare dinner.''

''Dad-dy—is.''

Tory pressed the ice-cold drink to her forehead, thinking about Slade's expertise in the kitchen, which consisted of boiling water and opening cans. ''He is?''

''Uncle Slade is getting pizza for dinner,'' Jamie piped in. ''Daddy and him are driving into town right now.''

''Where's Grandma and Grandpa?'' Judy asked, finishing the last of her lemonade.

''Grandma is still taking a nap. Grandpa is watching the news.'' Ashley grabbed her mother's arm. ''Come on. Daddy will be back soon with dinner. We were supposed to find you.''

Judy threw a helpless look toward Tory. ''I knew it was too good to last.''

Tory checked her watch. ''I guess thirty minutes is better than none.''

Mindy followed Ashley's lead and took hold of Tory's arm, pulling on her. ''Come—on.''

Tory blew a long sigh out between pursed lips. She'd wanted to explain to her sister about the sleeping arrangements but hadn't found the right words. They had sipped their drinks, stared at the horses in the paddock and hadn't said more than a few words in the past thirty minutes, relishing the silence instead.

''I believe our quiet time is up, sis,'' Judy said, laughing as her daughter tugged her toward the house almost at a jog.

Mindy and Tory took up the rear at a much slower pace. ''Jam-ee—calls—Dad-dy—Un-cle—Slade. Do—you—uh—'' she paused for a few seconds ''—think I—could—call—Ju-dy—Aunt?''

''She'd be flattered. We're all family now.''

''I've—been—think-ing. Can—I—call—you—Mom?''

Stunned, Tory halted in her tracks, tears springing to her eyes. She opened her mouth to say something but nothing came out. The question, spoken so casually, robbed her of coherent thought.

''If—you—don't—want—''

Tory swallowed several times. ''I would love for

you to call me Mom,'' she said, tears streaming down her face.

''Why—are—you—cry-ing?''

Tory smoothed back Mindy's hair, then swiped at the wet tracks running down her cheeks. ''Because you've made me so happy.''

''Do you—think—Dad-dy—will—care?''

Would he? Slade still had so much guilt over the car wreck that had taken his wife's life. Yes, he wanted Tory to help him raise Mindy, but even though they were married, she really didn't feel like his wife. They were housemates with a license declaring them husband and wife. That piece of paper was only one small part of it.

''Honey, you'll have to ask your father that. I can't answer for him.''

Mindy took her hand. ''Then—I will.'' She started for the house again.

Tory reached out to open the screen door when she heard a car coming down the lane toward the house. Slanting a look over her shoulder, she saw Slade and Brad pull up in front and climb out of the silver sedan. ''Dinner has arrived.''

''I—love—piz-za.''

''So do I. It's just never on any diet that I know of.''

''Diet?'' Slade carried five large boxes. ''What diet?''

''The diet I need to start after this weekend.''

Slade's gaze traveled slowly down Tory's length before reestablishing eye contact with her. ''Why? I don't see the need.''

Heat, having nothing to do with the ninety-degree temperature, flamed her cheeks. "I've been fixing more full-course meals than I usually eat. Trust me. I need to cut back."

"I like you just the way you are."

Slade's impish grin that curved his mouth curled her toes. "Pleasantly plump?" For a few seconds she'd forgotten that Brad and Mindy were standing close, listening to every word said.

"The pleasant part is right." Slade's grin grew to encompass his whole face, down to the twinkle in his eye.

Brad cleared his throat. "If we don't get these inside, they will be stone-cold."

"I—like—cold—piz-za, Uncle—Brad."

Everyone looked at Mindy, surprise on Brad's and Slade's faces. Tory watched Slade's reaction to what Mindy had said. His surprise quickly transformed into acceptance.

He thrust open the door, holding it for Mindy and Tory to enter the house first. "You might like cold pizza, but I don't."

"We probably should reheat them anyway. That's a fifteen-minute drive."

When Tory came into the kitchen, she immediately turned the oven on to four hundred degrees. Slade and Brad laid the five boxes down on the counter and quickly escaped to the back deck while the women reheated the pizza.

Outside, the house shaded the wooden deck, offering some relief from the temperature while a light breeze stirred the hot air, making it bearable. Jamie darted down the steps to the yard and dashed across to the tire swing. He conned Ashley into pushing him by promising he would do the same for her. Mindy stayed on the deck watching them from the railing.

Slade folded himself into a cedar lounge chair, stretching his legs out in front of him. ''Are you okay with Mindy calling you Uncle?''

''You bet.'' Brad sat next to him. ''You have a wonderful daughter.''

Slade's attention shifted to Mindy who braced herself against the railing. She was tired. He could tell by her drooping shoulders and the fact she hadn't joined the other two at the swing. Ever since Tory's family had arrived, his daughter had been going a mile a minute, trying to keep up with everyone. He longed for the day when she would race across the yard, leading the pack, instead of following slowly behind.

''I don't think I'll have any trouble getting her to go to bed tonight, especially with the kids camping outside. She's so excited about that.''

''Saturday after the carnival Judy and I are heading to Grand Lake to camp for a few days before we head home. Tory's parents are going back to Dallas. We would love to take Mindy along.''

''Camping? If she wants to go, that'll be fine with me. I can rearrange her therapy sessions if need be.''

''Ashley will be thrilled. She's been talking about taking Mindy with us. Jamie, too, even though she's just a girl, he said.''

The way Tory's family had taken Mindy into their

hearts only reconfirmed he'd made the right decision in marrying Tory. "Sweetheart?"

Mindy twisted around, looking at Slade.

"Would you like to go camping with Ashley and Jamie? They're going to Grand Lake for a few days."

A smile lit his daughter's face. "Yes!"

"Just as I thought," Slade said to Brad.

"It's my turn. Get off," Ashley shouted.

Brad surged to his feet. "Better take care of this before war is declared."

Slade patted the chair that Brad had vacated. "Come sit by me. Are you enjoying Ashley and Jamie's visit?"

Mindy came toward the lounge chair, her foot dragging more than usual. "Yes. They—are—uh—fun." She scooted back until her feet dangled over the edge. "Dad-dy, can—I ask—you—some-thing?"

"Sure, anything."

She clasped her hands together in her lap and studied them. "I—want—to—" she drew in a gulp of air "—call Tor-ee—Mom. Is—that—kay?" She swung her large gaze to his.

Okay? There was a part of him that was thrilled she wanted to call Tory Mom. But there was a part—where his guilt lay buried—that wanted to say no. Words crowded his throat, closing it.

Mindy's eyes grew round. "I—won't—if—you—don't—want me to."

Slade fought to keep his expression neutral while he brought his reeling emotions under control. His guilt affected so many aspects of his life. He needed to come to terms with it before it destroyed what was good in his life—Mindy and Tory. He wanted them to be a family. There was nothing else he could say but, "Honey, whatever you want is fine with me."

"I—love—Mom-my. But—I—love—Tor-ee, too."

He clasped his daughter's hands between his. "I know. You can love more than one person. Your life is always richer with people you care in it."

"Is—that—why—you—uh—uh—" Mindy pinched her lips together "—mar-ried—Tor-ee?"

"Tory is important to us both," he said, aware that Brad and his two children were walking toward them. When they came up the steps, Slade stood. "Tell Tory I needed to check on something down at the barn."

"But the pizza is—"

Slade strode from the deck and around the house, realizing his sudden disappearance would seem strange. But he had to be alone, at least for a few minutes while he put himself back together. His emotions lay frayed, the past few days having taken their toll on him.

He sought the quiet and coolness of the barn, walking to the far end. Leaning against the opening, he stared at the pasture beyond. One chestnut mare with her colt chewed on the grass on the other side of the fence. The sun had vanished behind the line of trees, bringing shadows to the landscape. The scent of earth, hay and horses swirled about him. A cardinal and its mate flew overhead and perched in the maple tree near the building. Serenity was all around him, and yet inside his emotions roiled, churning his stomach.

Tory was right. His guilt was ruling his life. That had to change if their marriage would ever have a chance. Was the Lord the answer? He'd never been good at praying, asking for what he needed. Was that why his prayers after the accident had gone unanswered?

''Slade, is there something wrong?''

He pivoted toward the sound of Tory's worried voice. She walked toward him, concern in her eyes. ''No,'' he answered. But when he continued to look at her, he said, ''Yes. Why are you here?''

''I know how much you like pizza, and when you didn't come in for dinner, I knew something was wrong. Brad told me you came down here. I thought maybe something happened that I needed to check on, too.''

He gestured to the area around him. ''Everything's fine.''

She came within a few feet of him. ''Then Mindy must have asked you.''

Surprised at how perceptive Tory could be, Slade turned away from her, not wanting her to read all his doubts in his expression. ''Yes, she did.''

''Is it okay?''

''I should ask you that question.''

''Of course, it's okay. I love Mindy like a daughter.''

The muscles in his shoulders and neck ached from holding himself so tense. ''Then it's okay with me. I told Mindy it was up to her.''

"But it bothers you?"

The waver in her question pierced his armor. He whirled about, needing to clarify his feelings not only to Tory but himself. "I was a little surprised, that's all. When I married you, I wanted us to become a family, but—"

"But you feel as though you've betrayed Carol?"

He nodded, his throat so tight he didn't think he could say one word.

"One of the things I like about you is your loyalty. Carol was your wife for seven years. You loved her. I don't expect those feelings to go away. We entered into this marriage for Mindy. We both love her." She took a step toward him. "It's okay, Slade, to continue living, to enjoy life. I'll keep some pizza for you. Come up whenever you're ready. I'll make sure no one bothers you until then."

He watched her walk away, her head held high, her shoulders back. He'd hurt her. Even though her expression hadn't shown it, he could tell by the dullness in her eyes. That had been the last thing he'd wanted to do. He couldn't continue like this.

Turning toward the pasture, he strode to the fence and climbed over it. In the field among the wildflowers, he slowly went around in a circle, taking in all the marvels of nature. God was everywhere. He needed God back in his life. He needed peace again.

He fell to his knees and bowed his head. *Dear Lord, please help me to overcome this guilt I feel for surviving when Carol didn't, when Mindy came away hurt. Please help me to move on in my life and to put the past behind me. I need to for Mindy's and Tory's sakes, but mostly for my own. In Jesus Christ, amen.*

"What's that sound?" Judy asked as she placed the last plate into the dishwasher.

"We have skunks under the house. They're fighting. Probably the male wants to move and the female wants to stay put." Tory dried her hands on the towel looped around the handle on the refrigerator.

"Skunks! When did this happen?"

"I'm not sure. Sometime in the spring. We thought we had a family of raccoons. We found out the hard way we didn't."

"You say 'we' so easily. Married life agrees with you."

Tory remembered her conversation with Slade earlier that evening in the barn. She thought it could, but how was she going to compete with a woman who was dead? She wanted her marriage to work, but she wasn't sure how to make that happen.

"Have you told him yet?"

"No. Why do you keep bringing it up? I want to forget about that part of my life."

"If it were that simple, you would have long ago. The very fact you haven't said anything to Slade about being raped tells me you haven't dealt with it." Her sister shut the dishwasher and turned it on. "Do you trust him?"

"If I didn't trust him, I wouldn't have married him."

"Then tell him."

"I will when the time is right." Whenever that

would be. She almost said something to him earlier in the barn, but the words wouldn't come out. Her past was as much a barrier to their marriage as his. What a pair they made!

"Do you think the men have gotten the children down yet?"

"In other words, do I think it's safe for us to come out of the kitchen?"

"Yep. Notice how fast I jumped at the chance to let them take care of the kids tonight? It's been a long day."

"Tell me about it. And tomorrow will be longer with setting up for the carnival on top of everything else." Tory headed for the living room. "Let's join Mom and Dad. I'm sure Slade and Brad have everything under control."

"I can tell you haven't been a mother for long or you wouldn't have said that."

When Tory entered the living room, her mother was cradled against her father's side on the couch, her eyes drifting closed. "Is she okay, Dad?"

He put his forefinger up to his lips, a plea in his eyes. "You two through with cleaning up?"

"Yep, and we got the easier of the two chores," Judy said as she settled into a chair across from the couch.

"Tsk, tsk. Putting children down to bed isn't a chore." The teasing light in their father's eyes dimmed when their mother murmured something and nestled closer to him.

"Dad?" Tory noticed the dark circles under her mother's eyes. It looked as if she wasn't sleeping well, but since she'd gotten here early this afternoon, that was about all she'd done.

Eleanor's head sagged even more, her chest rising and falling slowly as she sank into sleep. Tory's dad watched her for a few minutes before answering, "She hasn't been feeling well for the past couple of months. Tires easily. She goes to the doctor again next week when we get back. I'm afraid it's her heart."

"Why didn't you tell me?" Tory asked. "I knew she wasn't feeling well at the wedding, but I didn't know it had been going on for so long."

"I didn't want to worry you."

"Where my family is concerned, I don't want to be kept in the dark."

Her father's gaze drilled into her. "The same goes for you. Both your mother and I have wondered about this sudden marriage. We get a call one day inviting us to your wedding with no warning that you were even dating someone."

"I guess we all have our secrets."

"That's not what families do."

Her father pinned her with a probing look as though he could reach into her mind and see all her doubts about a good man marrying someone who might not be able to give him what he deserved. She started to tell her father the reasons behind her marrying Slade, but taking a look at her mother firmed her determination to keep quiet. He had enough to worry about without adding to his problems. All his married life he'd had a deep love for his wife. He wouldn't understand why she'd married Slade without that same kind of deep love.

The sound of the front door opening and closing alerted Tory to the men's return. She focused on the entrance, hoping her father didn't pursue the conversation, especially with Slade in the room.

When he and Brad entered, Tory laughed. "You two look like you wrestled a bear."

While tucking in his shirt, Slade exchanged a glance with Brad. "Three children who didn't want to go to bed are worse than a hungry bear." He ran a hand through his disheveled hair.

"Next time we'll let you ladies put the little darlings down while Slade and I clean up the kitchen."

"What took you all so long?" Judy asked, trying to contain her laughter behind her hand.

"First, I had to tell a story, then Slade. Then they wanted us to act our stories out. I'm exhausted." Brad plopped down onto the couch next to his father-in-law.

"If you think you're exhausted now, wait until the carnival." Tory shifted so that Slade could sit on the footrest to the chair she was using.

"So it doesn't look like there's any rest and relaxation with this vacation." Brad took a handkerchief from his pocket and wiped his brow.

"Who said vacations were for resting and relaxing?" Tory's father gently shook her mother awake.

"Obviously no one who knows the Alexander family," Brad grumbled, assisting his mother-in-law in standing.

"We're going to bed. It has been a long day for

us." Her father cradled her mother against him and walked toward the hall.

"That's our cue to turn in, too." Judy stood, offering her hand to Brad.

In under two minutes the living room was cleared except for Tory and Slade. Her gaze caught his, then dropped to her lap. The only place for him to sleep was on the living room couch or in her bedroom. Tomorrow morning she didn't want to explain to her family why Slade had slept on the couch. And yet, could she share a bed with him—her husband?

"I guess we should go to bed, too," she murmured, twisting her hands together.

Slade covered them. "Tory, nothing will happen you don't want to happen. That's a promise."

She believed him, but there was still a small part of her that would automatically panic. Closing her eyes, she prayed for strength to make it over this hurdle. It was important for their marriage.

She rose and extended her hand to him. He clasped hers and came to his feet. She faced him with only inches between them, so close their breaths merged.

"Why don't you get ready for bed first? I'll be along later. I want to check on the kids. Mindy's never camped out before."

Another stone in the wall around her heart crumbled. Sometimes she felt as though he could read her mind. The connection was disconcerting. "She'll be fine. Ashley will look out for her."

While she made her way to the bathroom, Slade left the house. She prepared for bed in less than fifteen minutes. By the time Slade came into the room, she was under the covers with the sheet pulled up to her chin. Since they had moved his clothing into her bedroom, he gathered his pajamas and headed for the bathroom, switching off the overhead light as he exited. All that lit the room were the slits of moonlight streaming through the slats in the blinds.

Tory clutched the sheet and stared at the dark ceiling. Her heart hammered against her chest while her pulse raced through her. An eternity later Slade reentered the bedroom, obviously feeling his way to the bed. She heard him crash into the nightstand and started to turn on the lamp on the table by her. Before she could, Slade eased down onto the mattress next to her.

"Good night, Tory." He rolled over onto his side away from her.

"Night," she managed to say.

Slade was her husband.

Slade was a good man and a wonderful father.

She trusted Slade.

Slowly her heartbeat returned to its normal pace and she released her death grip on the sheet. Slowly her muscles relaxed and her eyelids drooped. Sleep crept over her and she sank into the world of dreams.

Something hit his arm. A moan pierced his sleep-drenched mind. Slade's eyes bolted open.

Another moan sounded in the silence of the house. Tory twisted, kicking out at him. Pain shot up his leg. He scrambled away from her and came off the bed, reaching for the lamp.

"Don't. Please."

For a few seconds he halted his movements, thinking she was awake and knew he was going to turn on the light. But looking at Tory thrashing on the bed confirmed what he'd originally thought. She was asleep, caught in a nightmare. Flicking on the lamp, he blinked at the sudden brightness while Tory bolted straight up in bed, terror on her face.

Chapter Ten

Tory jerked the sheet up, gripping it in her fists. The sound of her heartbeat thundered in her ears. She knew Slade was speaking because his mouth moved, but for a few seconds she couldn't hear what he was saying. The suffocating compression around her chest threatened her next breaths. Pulling air into her lungs, she scooted back against the headboard.

"Tory? Are you all right?" Slade sat on the mattress, reaching out toward her.

She nodded, evading his touch to stand on the other side of the bed. Snatching up her robe, she stuffed her arms into the terry-cloth sleeves and belted it. The double-size mattress separated them, but it wasn't far enough away for Tory.

Flashes of her nightmare clung to her mind. The fear. The pain. The humiliation. Her body shook with the memories of four years ago—of the nightmare that plagued her when she allowed her fear to grow.

The concern on Slade's face tore further at her

fragile composure. She wanted to reassure him she was all right, but she couldn't get words past the constriction in her throat. Again she forced herself to inhale deeply until the crashing of her heart against her rib cage subsided.

When he started to round the end of the bed, she held up her hand and managed to say, "I'm okay."

Thankfully he stopped and studied her. If he had touched her, she was afraid she would have come unglued. She could still remember her assailant's hands on her, and the memory left her feeling unclean. She needed to shower.

Glancing at the bedside clock, she sighed when she saw it was nearly five in the morning. "I'm getting up. It's nearly time and I might as well get started on today's chores before the carnival committee comes out here to set up for tomorrow." Without waiting for him to say anything, she went to her closet and withdrew her clothes for the day.

As she crossed the room to the door, he finally said, "Tory, something frightened you. Do you want to talk about it?"

"No." She opened the door and escaped out into the hall.

The click of the door as Tory closed it reverberated through the bedroom, the sound bouncing off the walls and striking him with its finality. Slade stared at the wooden barrier between him and his wife. Until just a few minutes ago he'd thought they had made progress in their relationship. The nightmare was the answer, but she had locked the door and thrown the key away.

* * *

Exhaustion cleaved to every part of her. Tory took a moment to sit and regroup before the next set of children arrived to ride the horses. Perspiration plastered strands of her hair to her face and neck. She ran a towel across her forehead and around her neck but that did little to relieve the heat of a summer's day.

"Another hour and the carnival will be over," Judy said as she sat down beside her on the bale of hay in the shade of the barn. "This has been a roaring success. Everyone says so. They particularly like the horse rides for the children and young at heart."

The words her sister spoke barely registered on her numb mind. Tory closed her eyes and wished she could keep them closed for the next twenty-four hours. Sleep. She needed it badly. The night before she had lain next to Slade, listening to his even breathing and trying desperately not to fall asleep, not to dream again. She'd managed to stay awake most of the night and gotten up early again to do her chores before everyone else got up. Now, however, the lack of sleep the past forty-eight hours had caught up with her. She couldn't even lift her arms to brush a horsefly away.

"Tory? Are you with me?" Her sister waved her hand in front of Tory's eyes.

She blinked and offered her sister a smile. "Yes, barely. This has been a *really* long day."

"And it's not even three o'clock yet." Judy angled around to face her. "Mom and Dad have decided to leave this evening, too. Dad wants to get Mom back home."

"Yeah, he's worried about her. I'm worried about her."

"He's going to take her to the doctor as soon as he can."

"Good."

"And we'll leave right after them. We can get to Grand Lake before dark and set up camp. The kids want to go fishing first thing tomorrow morning. You two newlyweds will finally have the house all to yourself. You'll have peace and quiet for three days. Consider this one of my wedding presents to you, sister dear."

"Peace and quiet. I won't know what to do with myself."

"Do I need to give you a lecture on the birds and the bees?"

Tory hadn't thought beyond the fact she would have her bedroom to herself again and would be able to get a good night's sleep. But without Mindy in the house, she and Slade would be alone as husband and wife for the first time. He hadn't said anything to her about the nightmare, but he had kept his distance as though he weren't quite sure what to make of the situation.

That makes two of us, she thought, and shoved to her feet. "I think I hear the next group of kids. Ready?"

For the next hour Tory, with Judy's help, assisted children onto the saddle and led them around the riding ring. Some of them had been on horses before and rode without assistance. The laughs and smiles on the children's faces made the work worth it for

Tory. When the last one left and the cleanup crew went about dismantling the carnival booths and picking up the trash, Tory eased down on her front porch steps for a break.

Slade came out of the house and sat next to her. "Okay?"

"I'm not sure my feet are attached to my legs. But other than that, I'm fine."

"Mindy is almost packed and ready to go on her adventure, as she calls it."

"Has she ever been camping?"

"No, so I guess it is an adventure for her. She hasn't been fishing, either."

"She'll have a good time with Ashley and Jamie."

"You don't know how much it means to me that those two have taken a liking to my daughter."

"I think my niece and nephew are pretty lucky to have a friend and cousin like Mindy."

"The cleanup crew have promised me two more hours and no one will know we had a carnival here with a hundred visitors."

"It was a success. I think I'll offer again next year."

"Reverend Nelson was hoping you would."

Tory slanted a look at Slade, shielding her eyes from the glare of the sun. "You talked with Reverend Nelson?"

He nodded. "I told him I would be on the budget committee."

Tory's mouth fell open. "You did?"

"Yes. I've decided to start going with you and Mindy to church."

"When?"

"After our talk the other evening at the barn, I've been thinking. I was wrong to turn away from God just because something didn't happen the way I thought it should. I want to give Him another chance and hope He hasn't abandoned me."

Tory took his hand. "He hasn't. He doesn't work that way."

"I hope you're right because I can't do it alone. I realize my guilt has been getting in my way and I need to learn to deal with it. I hope He will help."

"He will." She squeezed his hand, then released it and rose. "I'd better go see if Dad and Mom need any help."

As she climbed the steps to the porch, his news lightened her heart and gave her hope. After the emotional turmoil of the past few days, she was glad for some good news.

Inside the air-conditioned house she relished the cool air while she made her way to the bedroom her parents had used. Her father slammed the suitcase closed as she entered the room. Her mother sat in the chair by the window, staring out at the workers cleaning up the grounds.

"Can I help with anything?"

"No, honey. I've got everything packed and ready to go." Her father placed the suitcase on the floor by the bed.

"I'm sorry, Tory, I haven't been feeling very well." Her mother turned her attention toward her.

She went to her mother and knelt in front of her.

"You never have to apologize for anything, Mom. I'm so glad you came to visit."

Her mother brushed back Tory's stray strands from her ponytail. "I know how much you hate coming home. This is the least I can do for you. The carnival was lovely again this year."

Her father came over to help her mother to her feet. She leaned heavily into him as he started for the door. Tory picked up the suitcase and followed them out to the car. Her throat tightened at the frail picture of her mother as her father helped her into the front seat.

While he stowed the suitcase in the trunk, Tory said, "Let me know what the doctor says."

"Of course, honey." He hugged her and kissed her on the forehead. "You have a good husband, Tory. I can rest easier now."

Slade approached her and stood at her side while her father started the engine, waved, then drove from the ranch. Tears misted her eyes. One fell and rolled down her cheek.

"Are you okay?" Slade wiped away the tear with his finger.

"Yes, but I just realized my parents are getting old."

"It's hard to watch the people we love becoming ill."

And he would know better than most, Tory thought as her father's car turned onto the highway and disappeared from view.

The sounds of children's voices followed by her sister's filled the air. The rest of her houseguests came down the steps, lugging their duffel bags. Brad carried Mindy's for her.

''Well, we're heading out now,'' Judy said as she tossed her bag into the back of the camper. ''You have my cell number?''

''Yes.''

''We're only two and a half hours away.''

''I know.''

''I'm not telling you but Slade.''

The paleness beneath his dark features emphasized how hard this would be for him to let Mindy go. Tory clasped his hand to convey her support as he watched his daughter climb into the camper.

He leaned toward her and whispered, ''Except for spending the night occasionally with you, I haven't been away from her since the accident. Three days is a long time.''

''You can always stop her from going.''

''Oh, yeah. That would be great. I'd never hear the end of that. Nope, I can do this.''

''Letting go is hard.''

''More than I thought. But she keeps telling me she's growing up.''

As the camper headed for the highway, Mindy waved, a huge grin on her face.

''This will be good for her.''

''I'll keep telling myself that over the next few days.'' Slade scanned the area where the carnival had been. ''They're almost done cleaning up. The place will be back to normal in no time.''

Normal? What was normal? A couple of months ago sharing a house with a man would have been so far from normal for her. She knew more than most how quickly life could change.

"I'll give the crew a hand. You need to rest, Tory. Take a nap. I know you haven't slept well the past few nights. Things will be back to normal in the house this evening, too. I'll take care of everything. I'll have my things moved back to my old bedroom."

It was hard for her to turn over the care of her ranch and animals to anyone, but she was too tired to argue. Besides, she had gotten good practice with Gus. "I think I'll lie down for a while or I won't make it to dinner."

"You didn't get enough junk food at the carnival?"

"Actually, except for the hamburger you brought me, I haven't had anything else to eat. Too busy with the horse rides."

"I should have helped you."

"If I'm not mistaken, Reverend Nelson had you supervising the races. When were you gonna help me? In between the sack race or the three-legged one?"

He turned her toward the house and nudged her forward. "Go. Take a nap. I'll fix something for dinner."

"I know I should be worried about that comment, but I don't have the energy to."

As she climbed the steps, she heard him say, "I can open a can of soup and fix a sandwich. I'm not that inept in the kitchen."

"I won't comment on that statement." She entered

the coolness of her house and made her way toward her bedroom.

In the room her gaze fell on Slade's pajama bottoms folded on the chair, an instant reminder of the past few nights sleeping in the same double bed as he. She'd known every time he had turned over or even moved a little. She'd listened to his soft breathing, surrounded by his scent that she'd come to know so well, and had yearned for things to be different.

She walked to the bed, its softness beckoning. As she sat, she caught a glimpse of Slade's Palm Pilot on the nightstand. Another sign of how much he'd become a part of her life in a short time. Easing back onto the pillow, she rolled onto her side and the second she closed her eyes, sleep descended…

The suffocating pressure of his weight squeezed the breath from her. Her ears rang from the blow to her head. Pain tore through her, wave after wave. Nausea rose to clog her throat.

In the dim light, his hideous face loomed over hers. ''You know you want it.'' His maniacal laughter rang out, underscoring how trapped she was.

''Please. Don't!'' she whispered through swollen lips, tasting the blood that pooled in her mouth.

A scream ripped from the depth of her soul…

Tory shot up. Darkness greeted her. Where was she? She could still hear the laughing taunt echoing in her mind. Arms came about her, drawing her against a hard body. Another scream welled up in her as she shoved away from the hard body.

''Tory!''

"Get away from me!" She scrambled off the bed and across the room, gasping for oxygen.

Lamplight flooded the room, revealing Slade on the other side of the bed, his expression a mixture of shock and concern. "You had another nightmare."

Inhale. Exhale. One breath at a time. She rubbed her temples as if that could rid her mind of the terror she'd lived with for four years, revisited each time she had her nightmare.

"Is it the same one?"

She looked up at Slade who thankfully kept his distance. Inhale. Exhale. She wasn't being raped. She was in her house, in her bedroom.

"Tory, I want to help you."

The soft plea in his voice unraveled the little control she was gaining over her composure. "You can't help." She crossed her arms over her chest, her hands sliding up and down her arms. But nothing she did warded off the chill burrowing into the marrow of her bones. She was so cold.

"What happened to you? What's behind these nightmares?"

She shook so much, she groped for the stuffed chair she knew was behind her and sat before she collapsed. She huddled back against the cushions, seeking some warmth from the cotton fabric.

He took a step toward her. Then another.

"Please. Don't!"

The words—the same she uttered in her nightmare—halted him. "Why won't you go home to Dallas?"

Tears flooded her eyes as suddenly as the light had

the room only moments before. "I can't. Too many memories of what happened."

"What, Tory?"

Through the sheen of tears she stared at him. In her mind she knew she should tell him what happened, but in her heart she couldn't find the words. She couldn't bear it if he—

"In God's eyes we are partners. What affects you affects me."

Sniffing, she brushed at her tears. "I know. I just have a difficult time talking about it."

"Did someone hurt you?"

In the depth of his eyes she saw compassion, understanding, and the dam on her memories broke. "I was raped four years ago. I was beaten up and put in the hospital by someone I knew and dated for a month. I never saw it coming until it was too late." She hunched forward, trying to draw in on herself, wishing she could make herself invisible.

"Where is he now?"

The steel thread in his voice caused her to look up at him. A nerve in his jaw twitched; his pupils were pinpoints. "In prison."

"Good. You pressed charges?"

She nodded, the pain and humiliation of the trial inundating her all over again. By the time it had been over she'd felt as if she'd been raped a second time but this time in public. After that she'd fled to Oklahoma and had never gone back to Dallas.

"Tory, you did nothing wrong."

"I went out with him. I thought I liked him. How could I have been so wrong?"

"Some people are quite good at putting up a front for others."

"Don't you understand? This makes me doubt my judgment about people."

"I know. But you must trust me on some level or you wouldn't have told me. That's a start."

"Is it? I don't know anymore. I'm so tired. I thought the nightmares were over. I hadn't had one in a long time."

"Until we had to share a bed?"

"Yes."

"I will never do anything you don't want me to."

"He kept telling me that I wanted it." The tears returned to blur her vision. She squeezed her eyes closed, trying to control her reeling emotions. She'd shed too many tears over that man, lost so much time because of the emotional scars his assault left on her.

"I almost have dinner ready. I was about to stir the soup when I heard you scream." He picked up his Palm Pilot. "I'm going to gather my things and move them back to the other bedroom now." When his arms were full of his clothing, he started for the door, saying, "I'll put these up and get the rest later. Why don't you come on into the kitchen and eat something?"

Tory drew in a deep breath. "What temperature did you put the soup on?"

"That burnt smell is from the toast for the sandwiches. The toaster was on too high and the first batch came out a little charred."

"I don't think that's it." She lumbered to her feet. "You put your clothing up while I check the soup."

Hot soup actually sounded good right now, she thought, walking toward the kitchen. The coldness was still embedded in her bones, and she hoped the soup would warm her up some. When she entered the room, her gaze went immediately to the stove where the contents of the pan were boiling all over the range top. Wisps of smoke drifted upward. She hurried across the kitchen and switched the burner off, shaking her head at the high setting Slade had put the soup on.

"Is the soup ruined?"

She spun about at the sound of his husky voice. "Yes."

"I knew you would be hungry. I thought high would get the soup done faster."

"There's some logic in that thinking, and it would have worked if you had been standing over the pan, watching it."

"And I would have, but I got sidetracked by a beautiful, caring lady."

The heat from a blush seared her cheeks. She busied herself by taking the pan to the sink and filling it with warm water. Then she used a sponge to wipe off as much of the burnt soup from the top of the stove as possible, considering the burner was still hot.

"I do appreciate you coming to my rescue." She sat at the table where the sandwiches were. She picked up the ham and cheese. "I thought you were toasting the bread."

"I decided against it and went with plain bread."

He slipped into the chair across from her as though he knew instinctively to keep his distance still.

"I'm gonna really have to give you some cooking lessons."

"That's okay. There are some things better left to the experts."

"It's not difficult."

"And I believe you, but—" He shrugged as though that gesture said it all.

"But you'd rather not learn."

"I just feel there are some things in life better off a mystery. Cooking is one of those things for me."

Tory laughed. "You're hopeless."

"I like that."

"That you're hopeless?"

"No, your laugh."

For a long moment her attention was totally focused on him to the exclusion of everything else. He was the one who made her laugh. He was the one who had given her a chance at a family. She owed him and wasn't sure how in the world to pay him back.

Chapter Eleven

Slade leaned against the railing of the deck, sipping his coffee. The hot summer air was still bearable at seven in the morning. The quiet would soon be disturbed by the sound of a bulldozer preparing the ground for the new indoor riding ring. But for the time being all Slade heard was an occasional bird, and he relished the silence.

Peace. He'd first moved out to the ranch because it had made sense because of Tory's work with the riding stable. Now he couldn't think of any other place he'd rather live. The sounds in the country were nature's sounds. And the best part was he only had to go twenty minutes to town. Not a long commute, and well worth it since Mindy loved living here.

A month had passed since Tory had told him about her past—a month in which he'd tried to court her and alleviate her concerns. In that time he'd realized he wanted their marriage to work on all levels. He was falling in love with her. That realization robbed him of his next breath. After Carol's death, he hadn't thought that would be possible. He hadn't wanted to open himself up to the kind of pain he'd suffered when she'd died. Now he knew it was too late. If Tory and he couldn't work through their problems, he wouldn't be able to avoid being hurt.

There were so many times he wanted to hold her, kiss her, and yet he held himself back, remembering that evening a month ago. She'd come unglued when he'd tried to comfort her after the nightmare. The terror on her face had scared him. Thank goodness the man responsible for putting that look on his wife's face was behind bars.

The bang of the back door alerted him to the fact that Tory had returned from the barn. He turned, fixed a smile of greeting on his face and handed her the cup of coffee he'd poured for her. "Everything okay with the horses?"

"Yes. Gus is worth his weight in gold. I can leave the ranch and not worry about it. I never felt that way before."

"Well, then maybe we should pay your parents a visit some long weekend."

She tensed, her hand bringing her cup to her mouth halting in midair. "I'm not ready to do that yet."

Until she was, he wasn't sure where their marriage stood. He took a long sip of his lukewarm coffee and saw the apprehension enter Tory's brown eyes. "Are you sure about Mindy returning to school?" he asked, deciding to change the topic of conversation before Tory retreated. They were good friends, but there still was a part of herself that she kept from him.

"I'm positive. You see how she is at church. She gets along with the other kids. Some of them will be at the same elementary school."

"But what if—"

She placed two fingers over his lips. "Shh. No buts. She's talking faster and is getting around well without any help. Right now she's at the barn talking Gus's ear off and helping him muck out a stall. I'm impressed with her progress."

When Tory removed her fingers from his mouth, he missed her touch. "So are her therapists and doctor. She's come a long way and part of the reason is you."

"Oh, my, you're gonna make my head swell if you keep saying things like that."

"I'm only telling the truth. Your riding program has been great for her. She's a pro on a horse now and so proud of it. She's talking about showing horses later down the line."

"I know. She's mentioned it to me a few thousand times."

"That's my girl. When she gets something in her head, she doesn't let it go."

"Which leads me back to the school issue. She wants to go very much. She loves being around people."

Slade threw up his hand. "Okay. You've convinced me. I know when I'm outnumbered."

"Good, because we need to go to school today and meet her teacher. I have an appointment for us."

"You do? You were awfully sure of yourself."

Tory grinned and finally sipped some of her coffee. "I've gotten to know you well these past few months. I was pretty sure I could talk you into it since it was so important to Mindy." One corner of her mouth hitched up even more. "Besides, I could always cancel if I had to."

"So you had all your bases covered."

"You know that Mindy will continue to need some special education services for a while?"

"Yes. Is the special education teacher who we're going to meet?"

"Actually, the woman will be her homeroom teacher. I think the special education teacher will be there, too."

He filled his lungs with air. "I guess I'm ready for this. Even with her tutor this year, she's behind."

"But gaining every day." She came to him, balancing her mug on the railing. "I promise you this will work. If there's a problem, we'll figure it out together."

He couldn't resist her nearness. He cupped her face, searching her features he dreamed about at night. "You don't know how much your support means to me."

"I could say the same thing. You've been more than understanding and I appreciate that, Slade."

Slowly he bent toward her, giving her plenty of time to pull away. She remained where she was only inches from him, her scent of lilacs mingling with the smells of the outdoors—earth, grass and the roses along the back of the house. He brushed his lips across hers, once, twice. Still she stayed put. That was all the encouragement he needed.

He wound his arms around her and brought her up against him, slanting his mouth over hers. Deepening the kiss, he became lost in her embrace, drowning in sensations he'd thought never to experience again.

When he parted, putting her at arm's length, he struggled to get his breathing under control. Her chest rose and fell rapidly, too. Pleased by her reaction to his kiss, he smiled, noticing how bright and blue the sky was, not a cloud visible.

"Lately I've been thinking, what do you say about adding on to the house?" He retrieved his now-cold coffee from the railing and finished the last few swallows.

"What?"

"Oh, another bedroom and bathroom. Maybe a den and a dining room."

"That would double the size of the house."

"Probably. What do you think?"

"We don't need another bedroom. We have three."

"But they are small. I was thinking about a master suite."

Tory's eyes widened. Her hand shook as she reached for her mug and brought it to her lips.

"I'm being optimistic, Tory. When we share a bedroom, the one you are in now is way too small. And I do believe the day will come when that will happen." After the kiss they shared, he knew it was only a matter of time. She responded to him. That had to mean something.

"I must admit the house is small. Better suited for one or two people, not three."

"Or, we could build a new house and leave this one for guests."

"A new house?" She pondered the concept, her brow creasing. "That might be better than trying to add on to this one."

"Think about it. In a few months I'll have more time and could help oversee its construction."

"Until the indoor riding ring is finished, I wouldn't want to take on another project."

"Mom—Dad-dy."

Mindy's voice sounded in the house, causing both of them to turn toward the back door. She rushed out onto the deck, dirt smudges on her cheeks, hay in her pigtails and something Slade didn't even want to know, on her tennis shoes.

"Is it time to go to school?" Mindy came to a halt in front of them.

"If it was, we'd have to wait until you took a shower. No way, young lady, will you go to school looking like that." Tory's nose wrinkled. "And smelling like that. What have you been doing? Rolling around in the hay?"

"Help-ing, Gus."

"I know, but—oh, never mind. Just go in and take a shower. Our appointment is at eight-thirty."

"Mom—I have—plenty—of time."

"Scoot." Tory waved her hands toward the door.

With a pout on her face, Mindy trudged back into the house.

"I've noticed she calls you Mom a lot."

Tory blushed. "I think she's just trying to get used to it."

"I don't think that's why."

She slanted a glance toward him, one brow quirked.

"She feels you're like a mother to her."

Tory beamed, her dark eyes shining. "And I feel like she's my daughter."

"We haven't talked about having more children. How do you feel about that?"

"I—I—" she swallowed several times "—I've always wanted a large family."

"So have I. Carol couldn't have any more children after Mindy was born. We wanted more and were thinking of adopting when the accident occurred."

The color drained from Tory's face. She twisted away and walked past him to the railing to stare in the distance. When Slade came up to her side, he could tell by the look in her eyes that she was wrestling with something. He waited, wondering if she would trust him with whatever was bothering her. Since she'd told him about the rape, she had opened up more to him. But there was still part of her held in reserve.

"I want children of my own. I just don't know how long I have. A few years ago the doctor said I would probably have to have a hysterectomy in my not-too-distant future. I have endometriosis and every year it gets worse."

"I see."

She spun about. "Do you really understand?"

"I think so. We both want a family, and if we are

gonna have that family, it needs to be soon. But you don't totally trust me yet. You're still not hundred percent sure about this marriage. Does that about sum it up?''

Tory nodded. ''I'm trying. Really, I am.''

The heavy thickness to her voice attested to the truth behind her words. Slade knew when it came to emotions a person couldn't always control things. He was still working through his own problems concerning the accident and Carol's death. How could he expect Tory to be over her ordeal and ready to settle down to be his wife in every sense of the word? No matter how much he wished she could get over what happened to her four years ago, it wasn't going to occur on his timetable, but on hers.

''I know you are, Tory.'' He took her hand. ''You don't flinch from my touch or run from me. I believe that's a good sign.'' He forced a lightness into his voice that he wished he felt.

''It was my lucky day when you brought Mindy out for her riding lesson.'' She inched closer, her face tilted up toward his.

Their gaze connected and everything around Slade faded from his awareness except the vibrant woman in front of him. His fingers delved into the rich thickness of her hair, for once loose about her shoulders.

''We—need—to leave.''

Tory jumped back as though caught doing something she shouldn't have. Her face became scarlet red and she busied herself by gathering up the two mugs and starting for the kitchen. "I need to change shoes and get my purse."

Slade looked at his daughter. He needed to talk to her about her timing.

"What are we going to do? We have a whole afternoon to ourselves." Slade switched on the engine to his car and pulled out of the church's parking lot.

"And you were worried about Mindy with the other kids."

"I guess I'll always worry about her. That's part of being a father."

"I have an idea what we can do."

"Nothing?"

"Nope. That does sound tempting, but I thought we might go for a ride."

"In the car?"

"No, you know very well I'm talking about riding a horse."

"That's what I was afraid of."

The laughter in his voice belied his words. She gave him an exasperated look. "I want to ride the new mare on the trail to the pond. Get her used to the terrain."

"Sure. You just want to see me ride again in all my glory." Slade came to a four-way stop sign and braked.

"You aren't bad."

"Yeah, I guess not. I can stay on the horse—as long as it goes at a sedate pace."

"So no racing across the meadow?"

"No way. Definitely out of my comfort zone."

"You know that needs to change. After all, I own

a riding stable and you are my husband. People will expect you to know how to ride well.''

His laughter rang in the car. ''I hate to be a disappointment to all those people.''

He started to ease out into the intersection when a car to his right sailed through the stop sign without coming to a halt. Slade slammed on his brakes, his eyes round as he watched the young teenager barrel down the road, not pausing in his haste to get wherever he was going.

Slade's grip on the steering wheel was white knuckled. His jaw clenched and he drew in calming breaths. ''Are you all right?''

''Are you?'' Tory touched his arm. Beneath her fingers, his muscles were bunched as though locked in place. ''I'm fine. The seat belt works great.''

He angled his head toward her, the darkness in his eyes reaching out to her. Then he firmed his mouth into a grim line and eased across the intersection. He didn't release his tight grip until he pulled into the lane leading to the ranch house. When he'd parked, he sank back, cushioning his head on the headrest. His hands shook as he removed them from the steering wheel.

''Thank goodness Mindy wasn't in the car,'' he whispered, his voice raw. ''She's doing so well, I'm afraid…'' His voice faded into the silence.

Tory's heart broke. She slid across the seat and took him into her embrace. ''That was an example of how precarious life can be. In a blink of an eye, everything can change.''

He pulled back to look at her. ''I'm glad not this

time. But you're right, which means we need to make the most of what we have."

"Live for the moment?"

"To a certain extent, but we should always have our thoughts on the future."

"Well, with that in mind, get changed and let's go for a ride. I still need to check out the new mare." She scooted back to her side of the car, aware of their close proximity that did strange things to her insides. She thrust open the door and tossed over her shoulder, "You have five minutes to change. The last one ready gets to cool down the horses."

With the challenge thrown down, Tory raced for the house, taking the steps two at a time. Slade pounded up to the porch and pushed past her once she'd unlocked the door. When she entered the coolness of the entry hall, he was nowhere to be seen. She heard the slamming of drawers and a closet door and quickened her own pace.

Four minutes, twenty seconds later, a knock sounded at her bedroom door. She threw it open, dressed in jeans, T-shirt and riding boots, and found Slade on the other side, similarly dressed.

His grin was lopsided. "I guess this means I won."

"You cheated."

"I did not."

"I had to open the door."

"Because you were the first one there. I can't help it if the key was hard to get out."

"I should have left it in the door," Tory muttered, and came out of her bedroom.

''Do you want to race to the barn?'' He waggled his eyebrows. ''Double or nothing.''

''I think I'll cut my losses. Your legs are definitely quite a bit longer than mine.''

''I'll give you a head start.''

''How much?'' She paused in the entry hall.

''Out the door and down the steps.''

Tory dug into her jeans pocket and fingered the house key. ''Okay.''

She hurried out the door and quickly locked the dead bolt before Slade realized what she was doing. She heard his shouts as she ran down the steps and across the yard.

When Slade finally arrived in the barn a moment later, he said, ''You play dirty, Tory Donaldson.''

''You didn't say I couldn't lock the door.''

''I had to go out the back door and around the house,'' he grumbled, but the frown on his face was a pretense if the twinkle in his eyes was any indication.

She clasped her hand over her heart. ''Poor Slade. I feel for you.''

''I get no sympathy.'' He scanned the barn. ''Which horse do I ride?''

''Black Charger.''

''I don't like that name. Isn't he the one you don't use with the children?''

Tory laughed. ''Only because he is so big. Perfect for you but for small kids he's too tall.''

''Sure. This from the woman who locks me in the house in order to win the race.''

''You have a key to the dead bolt.''

He exaggerated his frown and mumbled something under his breath. ''Bring on Black Charger. I have something to prove today.''

Tory saddled her new mare while Slade followed suit with his gelding. Then she led Buttercup out of the barn and mounted her. When Slade was on his horse, she started for the trail that led to the pond. The sun was high in the sky, bright and hot. A light, warm breeze cooled her cheeks and made the ride bearable until they got to the trees. In the shade of the woods Tory stopped and twisted around to see how Slade was doing.

He bounced along, his gelding doing a fast trot. He clutched his reins too tight and he sat too far back in the saddle. Halting the horse beside Tory's, he sagged forward.

''I think every bone in my body has been jarred.''

''Remind me to give you some riding lessons.''

''Now you tell me, when I still have to go all the way back to the barn.''

''Relax. You need to loosen your hold on the reins. The horse can't move his head. Sit forward some in the saddle. You're too far back. The more in tune with the horse, the better the ride.''

''Can I just hold on to the horn if he decides to bolt?''

''He won't. This is a pleasure ride.''

''Pleasure ride? Your idea of pleasure is very different from mine.''

''Come on. I'll go slow and easy the rest of the way to the pond. We'll let the horses graze a while before heading back.''

''If I get off this horse, I don't know if I'll ever get back on.''

Tory laughed, loving the teasing tone in his voice. He was enjoying himself as much as she was. She loved to ride, to be one with a horse. What would Slade do if she set her mare into a gallop? Probably panic.

One day she and Slade would race across the meadow. That picture popped into her mind with such clarity that she was surprised. And yet, the vision felt right. She now saw her life with Slade by her side. Maybe those children she wanted wasn't that far-fetched an idea.

She threw a glance over her shoulder to check on Slade. The grimace on his face made her smile. ''Relax. We're almost there.''

''We still have to go all the way back.''

''I can't believe a man who was determined to fight a family of skunks would feel that way.''

''If I remember correctly, I didn't win that battle. It wasn't until you had a professional come out that we got rid of the skunk family.''

''But you gave it your best shot.''

''All I can say is I hope they're enjoying their new home miles from us.''

''Skunks are so cute looking. It's a shame people feel that way about them being around.''

''You have to admit they have a wonderful defense.''

''It sure makes me pause going near one.'' Again she looked back toward Slade. ''But you on the other hand went toe-to-toe with the mama.''

"Hey, I had a hose in my hand and yards and yards of ground between me and her."

"Did you know a skunk's spray can reach across yards and yards?"

He rolled his eyes. "Now you tell me."

Tory left the trees behind. The glittering water beckoned. She nudged her mare a little faster, relishing the bright sunlight that bathed her face. It was a beautiful day, not a care to disturb her thoughts. When she neared the edge of the pond, she halted Buttercup and swung off her.

Slade came to a stop next to Tory. "I thought you weren't going to go faster than a walk."

"I couldn't resist." She smiled up at him and the world came to a grinding halt.

The sparkle in his eyes and the grin on his face sent her heart beating at a rapid pace. This man was important to her. He was offering her a second chance at the things she wanted in life. His patience with Mindy and her was unbelievable. Could she trust him with her heart, enough to be a wife in every sense?

His gaze left hers for a few seconds as he dismounted. When he reestablished eye contact, his reins fell toward the ground. He reached out and brushed her loose hair behind her ear, then cradled her cheek.

"You're beautiful, Tory."

She wanted to say something, but her throat seemed to close. He moved nearer. The feel of his palm against her skin, the blue gleam in his eyes, meant only for her, riveted her to the ground.

"I want you."

The husky words didn't send her into a panic. Instead, they caused her stomach to flip-flop. Was she ready to put the past completely behind her? To forget about her fears and surrender totally and willingly to another? When he touched her, she didn't feel dirty, used.

His other hand came up to frame her face. He inched forward and leaned toward her. When his mouth grazed hers, the last thing she wanted to do was push away. She went completely into his embrace while his lips settled over hers. This felt so right. He wouldn't hurt her. He wouldn't force her to give more than she wanted.

She stood locked in his arms, her head lying on his chest, for a long time. The quick tempo of his heartbeat matched hers. The warmth of his embrace went beyond comforting. She cuddled closer, enjoying the protective ring of his arms.

"I'm perfectly content to stay here all afternoon," Slade murmured against the top of her head. "But we need to pick Mindy up in an hour from Laurie's."

"Yes, and we still have the slow ride back to the barn and you'll have to cool down two horses." She leaned back.

"I protest that bet." His brow furrowed.

She smoothed the lines away. "Tell you what. I'll take care of Buttercup while you take care of Black Charger."

"And I'll take you and Mindy out to eat tonight. We'll celebrate."

"What?"

He waved his hand in the air. ''Oh, I don't know. How about what a beautiful day this is?''

''Sounds good to me. Race you to the barn?'' She started toward her mare.

He halted her progress with a hand on her arm. ''No way, Mrs. Donaldson. Remember, slow and easy. I'm a beginner. Maybe one day we can race back. But this isn't the day.''

''Chicken.''

''And proud of it. I know my limits.''

Tory waited until Slade mounted his gelding before getting up onto Buttercup. ''I'm impressed. It only took two attempts to mount him.''

''I'm a quick learner.''

The ride back was done in silence. Tory savored the quiet, letting her thoughts wander to what happened at the pond. He had told her she would decide, set the pace, and he'd been true to his word. Maybe this evening they could explore more of their relationship.

After taking care of the horses, Tory headed toward the house with Slade beside her. ''I need a shower before we pick up Mindy.''

''I could use one, too.''

His words, spoken casually, doubled her heartbeat. She slanted a look at him and realized his remark was an innocent one.

''I get dibs first.''

''Of course, beauty before brains.''

''I'm not even gonna touch that line.''

His laughter echoed through the house as Tory hurried toward her bedroom, grabbed her robe and disappeared into the bathroom. For four years she'd gotten used to being by herself. Now she couldn't imagine this house without others in it. But Slade was right. This place was too small, especially if their family ever grew. That thought brought a smile to her mouth as she stepped into the shower and quickly washed the smell of horse and sweat off her body.

After toweling dry, Tory slipped on her terry-cloth robe and belted it. She ran a brush through her long hair, remembering Slade once telling her he liked it down about her shoulders. Was that why she was wearing it like that more? The realization she wanted to please Slade gave her pause. She was falling in love. When had that sneaked up on her? If she was truthful with herself, it had started from the very beginning with his concern and passion for his daughter.

A knock at the door startled her out of her musing. "Yes?"

"There's a phone call for you from Judy."

"Tell her I'll call her back in a few minutes."

"You'd better answer it now."

His tone of voice warned her something was wrong. She thrust open the door, aware she was only wearing her robe, and took the portable phone from him. "Judy?"

"It's Mom. The ambulance just left. She's been taken to the hospital. She had a heart attack. You need to come to Dallas."

Chapter Twelve

Tory stood framed in the picture window at her parents' house, staring at the street where she'd grown up. Dusk settled over the landscape, forcing some of the neighbors to switch on their lights. She remained in the dark, needing its comfort and shield.

Dallas. When she'd left four years before, she'd never wanted to return, hoped she would never have to. Her mother's heart attack had changed all that, and now she was faced with the past. Across the street and two doors down was Brandon Clayton's parents' house. They had thought their son had done nothing wrong, that she had lied about the rape. They had been so vocal in their protest, even though she had ended up in the hospital overnight from a concussion and cracked ribs.

"Tory?"

She pivoted toward the sound of Slade's voice.

"I got the overnight bag down. You'll need to pack what your mother needs."

She'd promised her father she would get some things for her mother, but she hadn't realized how difficult it would be coming back to this street. "I'm gonna stay at the hospital tonight. You and Mindy can stay here or at Judy's." She walked toward her parents' bedroom, her hands trembling, her legs weak.

"Brad said something about taking Mindy home with him so she could see Ashley and Jamie. I'll stay with you."

"No, you don't have to," she said in a rush. At his raised brow, she continued in a slower voice. "Mindy's upset. She'll need you." She knew that argument would persuade him as no other.

"I guess then I'll stay with her."

"You should be with her as much as possible."

"Are you sure you don't want me to stay?"

No! I'm not sure about anything right now. "Yes." The wounds of the past lay open, festering with the memories she tried to forget.

Only the day before she'd thrown aside her defenses and had contemplated making her marriage real in every sense. But all the fear and doubts had resurfaced the minute Slade had turned his car down this street—actually, when she'd seen the skyline of Dallas in the distance.

Tory hurriedly stuffed into the overnight bag what her mother would need. She needed to get out of the house before she fell apart. She didn't to have time for that. Her mother needed her and she was determined to be there for her. She ran four years ago.

She wouldn't now no matter what turmoil she experienced.

Tory took the bag and left the bedroom to return to the living room where Slade was waiting. The worry and concern she'd seen in his eyes on more than once occasion was evident as he rose and reached for the suitcase. His fingers brushed hers. She snatched her hand away, interlocking her fingers to still their trembling.

The doorbell rang. Tory gasped at the intrusion. She looked toward the door but didn't move. Slade strode to it and pulled it open.

"May I help you?"

"How's Eleanor? I saw the car in the driveway and we all want to know how she's doing." The gray-haired woman gestured toward the houses on the street.

Mrs. Johnston. Tory closed her eyes for a few seconds before filling her lungs with a deep breath and heading for the door. "Mom's holding her own. They want to do triple bypass surgery on her as soon as she is stable and her condition is good."

"Oh, dear me. I was so worried when I saw the ambulance leave here yesterday afternoon." Mrs. Johnston peered around Slade, her gaze directed at Tory. "I didn't know if you would come home."

The censure in the woman's voice shredded Tory's composure. She dug her fingernails into her palms and counted to ten. Mrs. Johnston had been one of the doubters. She lived next door to Brandon's parents and let it be known she didn't believe Tory's version of the events. She schooled her features into a neutral expression and said, ‘‘Of course, I’d come home. Mom had a heart attack. She’ll have surgery tomorrow or the next day. I wouldn’t be any other place but beside her. Thank you, Mrs. Johnston, for inquiring about her health. I’ll tell her when I see her in a little while.’’

‘‘She can receive visitors?’’

‘‘Just family.’’

Mrs. Johnston’s sharp gaze shifted to Slade, her mouth pinched into a frown. She stuck out her hand toward him. ‘‘I’m a neighbor from across the street.’’

‘‘I’m Tory’s husband.’’ He shook the woman’s hand.

‘‘Ah, I remember your mother saying something about going to a wedding a few months ago.’’

‘‘That would have been mine.’’

‘‘You didn’t send out any invitations?’’

‘‘No, Mrs. Johnston. It was a quiet wedding with a few friends and family.’’

The woman snorted. ‘‘Tell your mother I’ll be up to see her when she can receive visitors.’’

Slade closed the front door as Mrs. Johnston stomped down the porch steps. Tory went to the picture window and watched the older woman make her way across the street and to Brandon’s parents’ house. She clenched her teeth and sucked in several deep breaths.

‘‘A charming neighbor. Did I detect an undertone there?’’

‘‘I always said you were intuitive. She doubted my story about being raped and voiced her opinion to whoever would listen. She only came over to check out who was here. Mom and she hadn't been on the friendliest terms since—'' Tory swallowed the rest of her words. She didn't want to go into the dynamics of the neighborhood right now.

''We've got everything. Let's get going. I'll drop you off at the hospital, make sure your mother is doing okay and go see how Mindy is doing.''

''Give Mindy a kiss for me.''

''I'll bring her to the hospital tomorrow morning. If I don't, she'll pester me until I do.''

Slade locked the door to her parents' house while she carried the overnight bag to the car. When he joined her, Tory noticed Mrs. Clayton out on her porch talking with Mrs. Johnston. Both women turned and stared at her as she slid into Slade's car. A shudder shivered up her spine. She had done nothing wrong, but they made her feel as though she had. When would she be able to put the rape behind her?

''Where's Slade?'' Judy asked, handing Tory another cup of coffee.

Tory watched Slade and Brad walk across the parking lot and climb into her brother-in-law's white SUV. ''He went to your house with Brad. I thought it best he stay there tonight with Mindy. I don't want her any more upset than she already is, and hospitals remind her too much of what she went through.'' The lights of Dallas shone in the dark hours of night. She turned from the large window in the waiting room, suddenly needing to sit down.

''You're a good mother, Tory. I hope you can have children before it's too late.''

Tory rolled her aching shoulders. It might already be too late. Coming back here brought forth all those feelings she had run from four years ago. She wouldn't be able to give her husband what she had dreamed of all her life. While her girlfriends in high school and college had had sex, she'd saved herself. And for what? For Brandon to take it by force—all those years obliterated in a single moment.

"I saw Mrs. Clayton today at the house."

Judy came to sit next to her. She took her hand. "Oh, sweetie, I'm sorry. I should have gone to get Mom's things. I wasn't thinking."

"Ashley and Jamie needed you. Besides, I should be able to go home and not worry about it."

"Did she say anything to you?"

"No, but Mrs. Johnston came over to see how Mom was doing. I think she really wanted to see how I was doing and to put in her barbs—again."

"Does Slade know?"

Tory hunched her shoulders, staring down at their clasped hands. "Yes. I told him when you took Mindy camping."

"Good. He had a right to know."

Tory jerked her head up and stabbed her sister with a look. "Why? It happened to me four years ago. Before I knew him."

"Frankly, Tory, because it has such power over you."

As close as she was to her sister, Judy didn't know the half of it. Tory withdrew her hand and bolted to her feet, restless, wanting just to forget everything. Why couldn't it be that simple? She didn't like what was happening to her all over again. The doubts. The fears.

"Tory, you've married a good man. Let him help you."

She wanted to shout, "He deserves better than me," but she kept the words deep inside, where they festered. "I don't want to talk about me. It's Mom I'm worried about."

"We'll know more in the morning. Hopefully the doctor will be able to operate on her and she can begin recovering."

"Let's pray." Tory bowed her head and folded her hands.

Tory stopped pacing and scanned the waiting room. She never wanted to see this place again. She'd lived here for the past few days, sleeping when she could on the hard blue sofa in the corner. She had never thought of herself as an impatient person until now. She felt like screaming in frustration.

Plowing her hand through her hair, she resumed her pacing. "When do you think we'll hear anything?"

Judy glanced at her watch. "It shouldn't be too much longer." She turned to her father. "Dad, do you want some coffee?"

He nodded, his face pale and deeply lined with exhaustion.

"Come on, Tory. You can help me bring some drinks back." Judy tugged on her arm to get her moving toward the door.

"But what if the doctor comes back soon?" Tory asked as she stepped out into the hospital corridor.

"A few minutes won't make any difference, and I think you need to get out of that room. You're driving everyone crazy with your pacing."

"Sorry, I'm restless."

"Personally, I don't know how you have any energy to put one foot in front of the other. We've all been up most of the past forty-eight hours."

"Can't sleep until I know Mom will make it through the surgery."

"Hence the reason I'm making you go with me. Did you see the looks that other family sent us?"

"I usually ride to get rid of this nervous energy, but I'm fresh out of any horses at the moment." Tory attempted a grin that immediately faded.

"Is Gus taking care of the ranch?"

"Yes, thank goodness for him. He's staying at the house and, from talking with him earlier today, loving every minute of it. He feels like he's on vacation from his daughter."

Judy entered the coffee shop and ordered hot coffee for herself, their father and Tory. Taking the tray, she started for the door.

"At least let me carry my own coffee," Tory said, plucking her cup from the tray, "since you wanted my help in getting the drinks."

"Slade and Brad should be back in a little while with the kids."

"I don't know if it's such a good idea for Mindy to be at the hospital. She has been upset ever since she heard about Mom."

"The kids will need to see for themselves Mom's okay."

"I know. But she has bad memories about the hospital."

"Honey, I know you want to protect her, but I think Slade's doing the right thing."

In the waiting room the surgeon who had operated on their mother stood with their father, speaking in low murmurs. The tension in her father's face had relaxed, sparking hope in Tory.

She hurried to the pair. "Dad? Is everything okay?"

Her father smiled, his blue eyes lighting. "She's going to be all right. The operation went well. Thank you, Dr. Richards." He shook the man's hand.

After the doctor left, her father collapsed into a chair, his shoulders sagging. "Thank you, Lord, for bringing my Eleanor through safely."

"Amen," both Tory and Judy said.

Tory sat on one side of her father while Judy took the other chair next to him and gave him his cup of coffee. His hand shook as he brought it to his lips.

"She made it. She made it," he murmured between sips.

"Dad, when can we see her?" Tory set her coffee on the table in front of her, too edgy to drink any more caffeine.

"Not too long. The nurse will let us know."

"Tor-ee?"

Tory glanced toward the door and smiled. Mindy hurried into the room and threw herself into Tory's arms. She kissed the top of the child's head and hugged her.

"Miss—you."

"And I missed you, young lady. How are you doing?" Tory pulled back to look into the child's face, smoothing her hair back.

"How's—Grand-ma?"

"She's gonna be fine. The operation was a success."

"Not—gonna—uh—die?"

Mindy's large eyes appealed to her, causing her chest to tighten. "No, baby. Grandma's going to be one hundred percent better." She hoped.

"Can—I see—her?"

"Soon." Tory caught sight of Slade standing back watching their exchange. She offered him a smile, her exhaustion beginning to take over. Her eyelids felt heavy, her movements slow, all the nervous energy drained from her.

"I'm glad to hear your mother is okay." Slade took the chair next to her, stretching his long legs out and crossing them at the ankle.

"Thank you," she murmured, then hugged Mindy to her, taking solace in the feel of the child in her arms.

There was a part of her that wanted to throw herself into his comforting embrace as Mindy had her, but her trip home had raised all her doubts and fears she'd begun to put to rest. Over the last month she'd thought she had moved past her memories to forge a new future. She'd been fooling herself.

When the nurse came into the room, she directed

Tory's father to where her mother was. Time moved slowly as Tory waited her turn to see her mother. Weariness had a strong grip on her now.

Mindy scooted over to sit where Tory's father had been. Swinging her legs, she asked, "Do you—think—Belle—misses me?"

"Gus is taking good care of her. It won't be long before you see her again. What have you, Ashley and Jamie been doing?"

"Watch-ing—movies." The child shrugged. "Play-ing—games. Not much." She looked up at Tory. "Been—uh—uh—worried."

"You don't need to worry anymore. Things will be back to normal in no time," Tory said with more conviction than she felt. She'd finally thought her life was on track, but this derailment made her wonder if she was heading in the right direction. Slade deserved more than she was afraid she could give him.

When Mindy wandered over to Ashley and Jamie and they began to play a card game, Tory shifted around to Slade. With his head back on the cushion, his eyes closed, she studied his strong features, relaxed for the moment. A lock of his hair curled on his forehead. Her fingers itched to brush it back into place. She balled her hands and refrained from touching him. She twisted around, trying to find a comfortable position in the hard chair.

When she peered at Slade again, his eyes were open and watching her. She swallowed several times, but her throat remained parched. For a few seconds she glimpsed a yearning in his gaze that nearly undid her. He cloaked his expression and straightened.

"Did you call your office this morning?"

He nodded, his gaze fixed on her.

"How's everything in Cimarron City? Okay?"

"Fine. I've been informed by my secretary that I have done such a good job of hiring a great team that they can manage without me for a while." He angled so his knees touched her leg, and he took her hands within his. "I will be here for you for as long as you need me. Everything back home will take care of itself. You only have to worry about your mother."

The concern in his expression struck at her composure. She wanted to fall apart in his arms, to cry for her mother, for her lost innocence. But the sounds of the others held her rigid, especially the voices of the children. She pulled her hands from his and stood on shaky legs. If she stayed near him, she would fall apart, and Mindy didn't need to see that.

Tory paced from one end of the room to the other. With his fingers steepled in front of his face and his elbows resting on the arms of the chair, Slade observed her flexing her hands then curling them into fists. He wanted to help, but every time he'd tried, she'd shut the door in his face. He wasn't sure what to do anymore.

He shoved himself to his feet and said to Mindy, "I'll be back in a minute, sweetheart."

"Sure Dad-dy." She glanced up from her cards, giving him a smile that showed her missing tooth.

When he left the waiting room, he headed straight for the chapel, not wanting to be gone long. But he needed a quiet place to talk with God, a place free of distractions.

In the small chapel Slade sat on the front pew, bowed his head and clasped his hands together. This was still so new to him. He had been out of practice for so long. Where to begin?

Suddenly the words filled his mind. *Lord, please help me to be there for Tory. I don't know what she needs anymore. I know what happened to her, but I still feel she is holding something back from me, keeping something buried deep inside her that is a barrier to any lasting relationship between us. Please show me what to do. Should I try to force the issue? Should I back off? What do I do?*

Tory's mother lay in the hospital bed, pale, the wrinkles on her face more prominent, but she was alive. Tory walked to her mother with Mindy and Slade on either side of her. Her mother's eyes fluttered open and she smiled, a faint upturn of her mouth.

Tory cupped her mother's hand between hers. "Mom—" The words choked in her throat.

"Grand-ma! You—kay?" Mindy leaned near Eleanor.

She licked her lips. "Now, I am." Her eyes closed for a few seconds, then she looked again at Mindy. "You've grown."

Mindy straightened to her full height. "Gus—says—at least—an inch."

"Mom, can I get you anything? Bring you anything from home?"

"No, just tired." Her eyes blinked closed. "Rest."

"I'll be back later, Mom."

Tory, Slade and Mindy started for the door when Eleanor whispered, "Slade."

He turned and went back to the bed. "Yes?"

"Thank you."

His brow wrinkled. "For what?"

She swallowed hard and glanced at Tory. "For bringing my baby home." Then her eyes shut and her head sagged to the side.

He bent down and kissed her on the cheek. "You're welcome."

Tory's swirling emotions collided with her exhaustion. She made it outside the room before collapsing back against the wall and hanging her head so Mindy wouldn't see the tears gathering in her eyes.

"Mindy, why don't you go find Ashley and Jamie?"

Tory heard Mindy walk away, her foot dragging slightly on the linoleum floor. Then Slade laid his hand on her shoulders and lifted her chin so she looked him straight in the eye.

"I'm taking you to your sister's. No more sleeping at the hospital. You need to sleep in a bed and get some rest or you won't be any good for your mother."

She didn't even have the energy to argue with him. He was right. She knew it even though she hated leaving her mother.

Slade walked with his arm around her to the waiting room where he called to Mindy. Together they left the hospital. The trip to Judy's house was a blur. When she arrived at her sister's, Slade immediately escorted her to a bedroom where she saw their suitcase and sat her on the bed.

"Take a nap. When you wake up, you can eat something then go back to sleep. You have two days' worth to make up."

"Aye, aye, captain." She wanted to salute but couldn't lift her hand. Instead, she fell back and let Slade remove her shoes and place her legs on the mattress. Then he covered her, kissed her on the forehead and pulled the drapes before leaving the bedroom.

The warmth and softness of the bed cocooned Tory in a safe haven. Someone touched her shoulder and shook her. She burrowed deeper, not wanting to open her eyes to the real world.

"Tor-ee—Mom—are you—all—right?"

The frightened tone penetrated Tory's sleep-groggy mind. Her eyes bolted open to find Mindy standing next to her, her face crunched into a frown. "I'm fine, honey. Just tired."

"Mindy, you know you weren't supposed to bother Tory." Slade strode into the room.

Mindy hung her head. "I know. I was—worried."

Tory reached up and cradled Mindy's face in her palm. "Don't be. I needed to catch up on some sleep." She looked toward the bedside clock and noticed it was nine o'clock. "Morning or night?"

Slade grinned. "Night. You haven't slept that long. Are you hungry?"

"Yes." She started to rise.

Slade motioned her back down. "I'll bring you a sandwich. You stay put and rest."

"But, Slade, I—"

He shook his head. "No arguments. You're still pale and you have dark circles under your eyes. A four-hour nap isn't nearly long enough to make up for two days without much sleep."

Her eyes drifted closed as the two left the room. Now that she was awake, her stomach was rumbling, and she realized she hadn't eaten much in the past two days, either. She'd mostly lived on caffeine to keep herself going. No food and lots of caffeine were not a good combination.

Ten minutes later she heard the door opening. She sat up as Slade came into the room with a tray. "You're spoiling me. I've never had dinner in bed. Actually, I've never had any meal in bed."

"Maybe the way I delivered it will help you to overlook the way I made the sandwich. I got carried away."

Tory laughed when she saw the layers of food between two pieces of bread. "You expect me to get that in my mouth?"

He lifted his shoulders, looking sheepishly at the plate with a three-inch-high sandwich on it. "You might want to remove some of the meat—or cheese—or lettuce—or—"

"I get the picture. You put everything on this except the kitchen sink."

"I wasn't sure what you wanted." He sat on the bed, facing her, the tray between them. "I probably should have cut it in half, too."

"Probably." Tory peeled back the top piece of bread and took off some sweet pickles, a slice of tomato, a slab of cheddar cheese and one layer of meat. Then she cut the smaller sandwich into two sections. Her stomach rumbled in the silence.

Slade glanced at her and grinned. "You're not hurrying fast enough for your stomach."

Tory opened her mouth wide and bit into the smaller version of her dinner. After washing it down with some ice water, she ate some more. She gestured toward the remains on the plate. "Please help yourself."

Slade popped two slices of sweet pickle into his mouth, then rose. "I'm gonna put Mindy down to bed. I'll be back for the tray in a little bit."

By the time Tory finished eating her dinner, Slade reentered the bedroom. "Where is everyone?"

"In bed."

"Already?"

"You have to admit it has been a long day. Even Ashley and Jamie have gone to bed."

"Good. Judy needs her sleep as much as I do." Tory covered her mouth and yawned.

Slade retrieved the tray, saying as he made his way to the door, "I'll be back."

Tory slipped out of the bed when he closed the door and rummaged around in her suitcase for her pajamas. She used the bathroom off the bedroom to scrub her face and brush her teeth. When she inspected herself in the mirror, she could understand Slade's concern. She combed her fingers through her messy hair and flipped it behind her shoulders before leaving.

Slade came back, dug his pajama bottoms out of the suitcase and went into the bathroom after her. Tory got into bed and pulled the sheet up, reminded of the Fourth of July weekend when Slade and she had shared a bedroom.

"I know this has been a difficult few days for you, Tory. If you want to talk, I'm here." Slade sat on his side of the bed.

"Is Mindy all right now that Mom will be okay?"

"I think so. She said a prayer for her tonight. Also for you."

"For me?"

"Because you were sad." Slade's gaze snared hers. "Tory, keeping things bottled up inside of you isn't good. I want to help you, but I figure there's a lot I don't know about what happened four years ago."

Tory grew rigid. "What do you mean?"

"The other day with Mrs. Johnston. The undertone of the conversation was tension-filled. Why?"

"Because she didn't think Brandon did anything wrong. She thought I had made up that story about the rape. After all, we were dating. Had been for over a month." Tory balled the sheet into her hands.

"Was she the only one?"

Tory stared at her fingers twisting the cotton material into a wad. "No. Several others voiced their opinions, too." The memories of the gossip that spread about her inundated her. Her throat closed, tears stinging her eyes. ''Having a concussion and a few cracked ribs weren't enough for some people. I guess they wanted me battered, near death. In their eyes Brandon was a nice young man from a good Christian family. So it must have been my fault somehow.'' She lifted her tear-saturated gaze to his.

''Tory, I'm so sorry some people are narrow-minded.'' A nerve twitching in his jawline, he gathered her into his arms and pressed her against his T-shirt-clad chest.

For a few seconds Tory allowed herself to seek comfort in his embrace, his hand stroking the length of her back. Then their intimate situation engulfed her in sensations she wasn't ready to experience, not when she could replay all the hurtful things said about her. Panic surged to the foreground. She wedged her arms up between them and shoved away.

''No!'' She scrambled from the bed and snatched up her robe. ''Please, I'll sleep on the couch in the den. This won't work.''

Tory fled the bedroom. Her heartbeat hammered against her rib cage while her breathing became shallow gasps. She escaped into the den, the silence of the house a balm that sought to soothe her tattered nerves. Thank goodness Slade hadn't followed her. She couldn't have handled a confrontation with all that had happened lately.

Using a throw pillow to cushion her head, she curled up on the couch and tried to sleep. But in her mind's eye all she could see was Mrs. Clayton the other day watching her with a narrowed gaze and an expression of contempt. Tory had done nothing wrong, so why did she feel so dirty and humiliated? But memories of Brandon's trial only confirmed those feelings. There had been times she felt she had been on trial instead of him.

Tory twisted on the couch, trying to get comfortable. In the dark she saw the digital clock tick off minutes—way too slowly. Around four she finally surrendered to sleep, exhaustion overcoming her racing mind.

Tory bolted straight up on the couch when she heard a knock at the den door. "Come in." Swinging her legs to the floor, she ran her fingers through her hair and straightened her pajamas and robe.

Slade stood framed in the doorway, no expression on his face. "I wanted to tell you that Mindy and I are leaving for Cimarron City in a few minutes. I can't keep acting like everything is all right between us when it isn't."

Chapter Thirteen

Tory chewed on her lower lip. Slade was right. Everything in their life wasn't okay. The threads of their marriage were fragile.

"I'm leaving my car for you. I've rented one to drive back to Cimarron City. It was delivered a few minutes ago. Mindy needs to be back home in her normal routine. You need time alone. Maybe talk to your sister. Heaven knows, I've tried to get you to talk to me, to let me into your life. I know this isn't the best timing, but I don't think there ever would be a good time." He turned to leave, then looked back over his shoulder at her. "Figure out what you want. I'll be at the ranch with Mindy. I have some figuring out to do myself."

Tory opened her mouth to stop him, but the closing of the door reverberated through her mind. So final.

She pushed to her feet, but her legs shook so much she sank back onto the couch. There was a part of her that wanted to stay in the den and hide. But the stronger part demanded she get up and at least say goodbye to Mindy. The child didn't need to be hurt by what was going on between her father and Tory.

Tory again rose, taking a moment to get her bearings. Then she strode from the room. She found Mindy and Slade in the entrance hall saying their goodbyes to Judy and Brad.

Mindy came over to Tory and took her hand. "I'll—take—real good—care—of Belle—for you."

Tory drew the child into her embrace. "I know you and your dad will. The ranch couldn't be in better hands." She kissed her on the forehead. "Remember I love you, Mindy."

"I—love—you."

Tory lifted her gaze to Slade's and the tormented look in his eyes nearly unraveled what composure she had. "I'll see you two soon."

Slade's raised eyebrows spoke of his doubts. "We'll call to let you know we've arrived safely." He grabbed his suitcase and turned toward the front door.

"Thanks," Tory murmured as she watched the two leave her sister's house.

The ache in her heart grew the farther away Slade and Mindy were. Her chest hurt when she drew in a deep breath. Why did she feel as though she would never see them again?

Panicked by that thought, she started forward. Slade pulled away from the curb. Her face pressed against the window, Mindy waved to Tory.

She returned her daughter's wave, tears flooding

her eyes. *You're making a mistake letting him leave. He's the best thing that's happened to you.*

That was the problem. She did feel that way. But she didn't know if she was the best thing for Slade.

Her sister clamped her arm about Tory's shoulder. "Okay, you and I need to talk. Something is definitely wrong and I don't want to hear 'Everything's okay.'"

Tory cocked her head around to look at Judy. "Maybe I don't want to talk about it."

"I'm not accepting that. You need to talk about it. You keep too much inside, sis. Come on in and we'll have a couple of cups of coffee. Whatever it takes." With her arm still around Tory, Judy directed her toward the kitchen.

"Don't you think we should get to the hospital?"

"Nope. Not until you and I have that talk." Judy poured two mugs full of black coffee, then gave Tory hers. "Sit."

"All this bossing around reminds me of when we were kids."

Judy sat across from Tory. "And changing the subject will not work. What's going on with you and Slade? Why were you sleeping in the den?"

Tory took in the stubborn set to her sister's face and knew she wouldn't be allowed to leave until they had discussed at least some of what was happening in her marriage.

"I see those wheels turning, Tory. You're trying to figure out how much you can get away with not telling me. Let me help you get started. How much has coming back to Dallas affected you? I know you never wanted to return. And frankly, after the way some people treated you, I don't blame you.'' With her elbow on the table, Judy planted her chin on her fist and waited.

Tory raised the mug to her lips and took a long sip. ''A lot. As long as I didn't see people like Mrs. Clayton and Mrs. Johnston, I could pretend I was fine, that I'd put everything behind me. But, Judy, I saw the contempt in their faces. I felt all over again the humiliation and condemnation I experienced back then. I felt dirty, as though I had been in the wrong, not Brandon. I know I shouldn't feel that way, but we had been dating. What if I le—''

Judy brought the flat of her hand down onto the wooden table. The sound echoed through the kitchen and caused Tory to flinch.

''Don't you dare start doubting yourself. You did nothing wrong.''

Tory pointed to her head. ''I know that in here.'' Then she laid her hand over her heart. ''But I can't seem to grasp it in here.''

''I have someone I want you to talk to.'' Judy went to the counter and grabbed a notepad and a pen. After scribbling on the paper, she tore it off and handed it to Tory. ''We will continue this conversation after you see Susan Conway.''

''Now?''

Judy checked her watch. ''Yes, she should be home. She's a stay-at-home mom. I'll call her to tell her you're coming to see her.''

''Why?''

"I want her to tell you. It isn't my place. Go talk to her."

"What about Mom?"

"Mom would be the first person to tell you to take care of this before anything else. You can see her later. This is too important to your future."

Future? Tory wasn't sure what kind of future she had. Slade had left with Mindy, disappointed and upset with her. And she couldn't really blame him.

Fifteen minutes later Tory rang Susan Conway's doorbell. A young, attractive woman answered the door with a smile.

"Come in. Judy called me. For some time I've wanted to meet you and thank you." Susan directed Tory into her living room and gestured for her to have a seat on the couch.

"Thank me? For what?"

"For doing something I couldn't. For being braver than I could be."

"Brave? Me?" Right now she didn't feel that way.

Susan sat across from Tory in a wingback chair. "Let me tell you a story. Maybe then you'll understand. Six years ago I was a freshman in college and ready to take the world by storm. I'd never been away from home, but I was confident I could handle anything. That was true until I dated Brandon Clayton."

Tory's breath caught in her throat, contracting it. She straightened, every muscle locked.

Susan's gaze fell away as she continued. "We'd been dating about three weeks. I thought I was so lucky because he was older and quite popular on campus. My roommate couldn't believe a senior was interested in me. I guess he thought I would do anything he wanted. When I wouldn't, he forced himself on me and left me battered and bruised physically as well as emotionally."

"But if he—"

Susan's tear-filled gaze reconnected with Tory's. "I didn't report the rape. I was too ashamed and just wanted to forget it ever happened."

Tory pushed her own feelings of shame aside and said, "But he hurt you!"

"At the time I thought maybe I'd done something wrong, something to provoke the assault. I dropped out of college and went home to lick my wounds." A tear rolled down her face. "But you didn't. You made him pay for what he did to you. I followed your trial closely and cheered when the verdict came in."

Tory slid her eyes shut, wishing she'd known about Susan four years ago.

"When I finally got up enough nerve to meet you and tell you about what happened to me, you were gone. It wasn't until later that I met your sister at church. Recently when I heard about your wedding, I told her about what happened to me and that I was glad you were able to move on with your life. She's the only other person who knew about my rape except my husband and now you."

"I wish I'd have known years ago. I thought I might have done something wrong."

"I know I've been a coward. I didn't realize until

recently that part of my healing was because of you. I knew I hadn't done something wrong, that he had because he did it to another woman."

Tory started to speak, couldn't and cleared her throat. "I wonder if there are others like us."

"I feel sure there are. Brandon Clayton is a sick man. He was handsome and charming on the surface, but that was as far as it went. You were the only brave one of us to come forward. And for that I thank you. May God bless you for many years to come."

Despite the heat outside the car, Tory switched off the air conditioner and rolled down all the windows. She wanted to feel the wind, to smell the fresh air. She wanted to remember she was alive and well with a husband and daughter waiting at home. She had a family whether she had any biological children or not.

Brandon Clayton hadn't taken away what she wanted more than anything in the world. God had brought to her doorstep a man who loved her even knowing her past. Why had she been so afraid to give herself totally to him? Yes, Brandon had taken her virginity away, something she'd wanted to give to her husband. But that was only a small part of her.

The wind felt warm against her skin, and Tory cherished the feeling as she headed her car toward Cimarron City and her ranch—their ranch. She'd spent another hour with Susan Conway, talking about their ordeals, emotionally washing themselves clean of Brandon's mark. They had prayed afterward, then hugged goodbye. When she had left Susan's house, she'd felt like a new woman, a free woman.

Suddenly the months with Slade took on a new meaning. He'd never once tried anything she hadn't wanted. He'd become her friend and confidant. He'd taken her house and turned it into a real home while she'd held on to her fear and shame. She'd let Brandon Clayton rule her life for the last time.

When she pulled into the lane that led to her house, her heart quickened its beating. Her mouth went dry. What if he and Mindy weren't there. What if he'd decided their marriage wasn't worth it? What if—? She shook the doubts from her mind. She was through doubting herself. She would fight for what she wanted most—to be Slade's wife and to have a family.

She parked in front of the house, hopped out of the car and hurried toward the porch. The sun's last rays were fading in the western sky. Dark shadows crept closer, but the lights on in the living room attested to someone being home. Her foot took the first step. The screen door flew open and Mindy came out.

"Mom, you're—home!" Mindy rushed at her, throwing herself into her arms. "I—missed—you."

Tory tousled the child's hair. "It was only a day. I had to make sure Mom would be all right before coming home." The word *home* rang in the warm summer air, loud and clear, a declaration of her feelings.

When Tory looked toward the door, Slade stood framed in the entrance to the house, his face hidden in the shadows of evening. "The doctor said Mom's operation was a complete success. She should be getting better each day. She sends her love.''

''Mindy, it's been a long day and you have school tomorrow. You need to get ready for bed.''

Mindy spun about, her hands on her waist. ''But—Dad-dy.''

Slade held the screen door open and moved to the side. ''Scoot, young lady. Now. Tory and I will be in to say good-night in a few minutes.''

When the screen door banged closed behind Mindy, Slade said, ''I'm glad your mother is getting better. Judy called earlier to tell me you were on your way home.''

''I asked her to let you know.''

''Why didn't you call?''

Even though she'd sat in a car for the past four hours, she needed to sit down to stop the trembling in her legs. She eased onto the swing, leaving enough room for Slade. He took the chair across from her, his expression still obscured by the growing darkness.

Tory clasped her hands together. ''What I have to say to you can't be done over the phone.'' She glanced out into the yard, barely making out the dark line of trees to the west. ''No, that isn't the complete truth. I was scared.''

''Why?''

There was no emotion in that one word and it sent a tremor down Tory's length. ''Because I thought you might not be here. Because I didn't want to hear the anger in your voice. Because I've become a coward.''

''Coward? You aren't a coward.''

The incredulous tone to his voice prompted a smile. ''Oh, yes, I am. Four years ago I stood up for myself and it nearly destroyed me. I've been running ever since, hiding from the past, hiding from my feelings. Not anymore.''

''What happened to change your mind?''

She saw the stiff set to his body, as though he were frozen. ''You and Mindy. It took the threat of losing you two to force me to do some thinking. I had a long talk with a woman who helped me to see what I'd done. She thanked me for going to the police about Brandon Clayton. She hadn't been able to, but she was glad he was serving time for what he'd done.''

Some of the tension drained from Slade. He leaned forward, resting his elbows on his knees, his face cast in the light streaming through the partially open drapes in the living room. ''He'd raped another woman?''

''Yes.''

Slade's hands curled into fists, then flexed. ''Good thing he's in prison.''

''She made me look at the whole ordeal of the rape and trial in a new light. I was wronged and I fought back. I have nothing to be ashamed of.''

Slade surged to his feet and sat next to her on the swing, gripping her hand. ''Ashamed? There is so much about you I admire. You have no reason to feel that way.''

''That's easier said than done. I never shared everything with you. But that's gonna change starting now.'' She twisted so she faced him on the swing, their hands still linked. ''I was saving myself for my husband. When I was a teenager, I'd made that decision. It had become very important to me as an expression of my love. Brandon took that away from me. He shattered a dream. He'd taken the decision out of my control.''

Slade's fingers about hers tightened. ''I know what it's like not to feel like you have any control over a situation.''

''Then you understand?''

He nodded. ''When I had that wreck, my life changed instantly. I learned firsthand how little control we really have over our lives.''

''That's why faith in God is so important.''

''I believe that now, but at the time I was angry and lashed out at myself, at God, at the Fates.''

''My faith was the only thing that kept me going. I ran from my family. I wouldn't let them support me. I hid out here and licked my wounds, pretending everything was normal. It wasn't.'' Tory grasped Slade's other hand, too. ''I wouldn't let a man touch me. I didn't like even getting near a man, and certainly being alone with one panicked me.''

''You're alone with me. I'm touching you.''

''That's just it. You don't threaten me. I let down my guard enough to really get to know you and what kind of man you are. I knew you would never hurt me. That's why I could agree to marry you and provide Mindy with a home.''

He smiled. ''I'm glad you realized that. I'd never hurt you.''

Tory moved closer, their knees touching on the swing. "I wanted more and thought I was ready for it. Then we had to go to Dallas and all my memories of what happened slapped me in the face. Now I realize that if it hadn't been Dallas, something else would have triggered the buried feelings. I had to deal with them, not run from them."

"Have you stopped running?"

She leaned toward him. "Yes, definitely. I love you, Slade Donaldson, and I want us to be husband and wife in every sense."

His lips met hers in a gentle kiss. "I love you, Tory Donaldson."

"Let's go say good-night to Mindy before she wonders what happened to us."

Slade grasped Tory's hand as they walked into the house. The comfort of his touch melted any doubts she might still have. When they entered Mindy's bedroom, she was in her bed with the pillows propped up behind her back and a book in her lap.

"Dad-dy start-ed *Black—Beau-ty.*"

"I loved that book when I was a little girl."

Tory sat at the end of the bed while Slade scooted a chair close to Mindy. He began to read, his deep, baritone voice floating to Tory and enveloping her in its rich tones that she wanted to hear every day of the rest of her life.

When he finished the chapter, he snapped the book closed and put it on the nightstand. "Good night, sweetheart."

Mindy snuggled down into the covers while Tory arranged them around her and Belle. "I'm so glad to be home. After school tomorrow, you and I will go for a ride."

"Yes! Dad-dy, too?"

Tory slanted a look back at Slade. "Daddy, too. That is, if he can come home early from work."

"You two have a date," he said, lounging against the doorjamb.

Tory brushed a kiss across Mindy's forehead, then switched off the lamp on the nightstand. The light from the hallway illuminated her way toward Slade silhouetted in the doorway, relaxed as though he had not a care in the world.

In the hallway by her bedroom Slade drew her into his arms, his mouth claiming hers. When he pulled back, he whispered, "I love you, Tory," then gave her a quick kiss on the lips before releasing her and heading toward his bedroom.

Dazed, Tory watched him walk away. "But what about—"

He swung around, his hand on his doorknob. "As I told you before, you're in control. You're calling the shots. The next step is up to you."

The quiet click of his door as he closed it resounded in the hall. The silence of the house cloaked her in a feeling of safety. She glanced at her door then at his. Chewing on her bottom lip, she thought about her ride to the ranch, about her conversations earlier with Susan and Slade and knew what she wanted to do more than anything. She walked to his door and pushed it open.

He turned toward her, a smile of welcome on his face. She shut the door and flew into his embrace.

Epilogue

Mindy rushed into the spacious new kitchen decorated in palm trees and bamboo with red and green accents. She came to a halt beside Tory at the counter. ''Laurie's here. She's the last one. Come on. I can't open my presents without you, Mom.''

''Whoa. Slow down. I'm just about through with putting the punch together.'' Tory dumped the frozen lemonade into the large pitcher and stirred the liquid with a wooden spoon.

''Mom! We all want to ride.''

Tory grinned and laid the spoon in the sink. ''I know, but first the presents then the food. Is your dad ready with the video camera?''

Mindy cocked her head. ''What do you think? Does he go anywhere without it?''

''Not lately,'' Tory said with a laugh. ''You go back to your guests and I'll be right there.''

''Promise?''

''Have I ever let you down?''

Mindy shook her head and hurried back into the den.

Tory swung around and scooped up Sean from the high chair. Banana bits were all over his mouth and the front of his shirt and even in his dark hair. ''You are one messy eater, young man.'' She took a washcloth and wiped him clean. ''We'd better get into the den. Your big sister is impatient. Maybe you can ride today, too. Of course, it will have to be with your daddy.''

Sean grinned up at her and made babbling sounds as though he were telling her that would be fine by him.

The second Tory entered the den, Mindy tore into the first present in front of her. Sean played with one of Tory's buttons on her shirt while his sister opened one gift after another to the excitement of ten little girls from her class.

Slade moved to Tory's side, smiling at Sean. ''Are you sure Gus is up to this? Eleven screaming girls may be too much for him.''

''Are you kidding? He's gonna love every minute. He adores Mindy and anything she wants, she gets.''

''Maybe I should rephrase the question. Are you and I gonna be up for eleven screaming girls trying to ride?''

''They're not screaming. They're just enthusiastic.''

''Is that what you call this?'' he shouted above the din. ''I think they're all trying to talk at once.''

Tory took a whiff. ''I think our son needs to be changed.''

"I'll trade you. You film this free-for-all while I change Sean."

"Oh, a man after my own heart." Tory patted her chest.

"Since you have mine, it's only fair I have yours." His mouth whispered across Tory's right before he plucked his son from her arms and gave her the video camera. "Don't aim directly at the windows. Too much light."

"Aye, aye, Captain."

She watched as Slade lifted his son high in the air and swung him back and forth. Sean's peals of laughter mingled with the chattering racket behind Tory. Her heart swelled as she took in the scene in the den. This was her family. It couldn't get any better than this.

* * * * *

Dear Reader,

A Family for Tory is centered around a therapeutic riding stable. I have had the good fortune to be involved with one and have seen the smiles on the children's faces when they ride. Children benefit so much from being around animals. I am continually amazed at how God has provided ways for us to heal from emotional scars as well as physical ones. I have tried to show some of them in this book.

Tory must learn to trust again and to let go of her fear. Slade must forgive himself for surviving a wreck while his wife didn't and his daughter ended up injured. Mindy must relearn some of the simplest things in life because of her surgery. The three of them with God's help become a family and help each other to heal.

I love hearing from readers. You can contact me at P.O. Box 2074, Tulsa, OK 74101 or Mdaley50@aol.com.

May God bless you,

Margaret Daley